WICKERMAN

CAPERS

GIRI KURICHIYATH

Copyright © Giri Kurichiyath, 2023

CONTENTS

THE SPOTTED TIGER

It was a Sunday morning, although it could have been any morning. Vikraman was sitting in a deckchair on the porch of his house, teaching Chimban, his kitten - a tiny, grey, furry affair with an upright tail and big curious eyes - how to play soccer with a ball of paper tied to a thread, when Manoharan appeared bearing an expression of extreme optimism.

Vikraman looked up.

Chimban capitalized on the distraction. He ran with the ball and deftly executed an own goal.

"I've written us into an adventure," Manoharan said and snapped his fingers beckoningly at Chimban.

Vikraman frowned. That was bad news. The ignoramus couldn't even read, let alone write anyone into an adventure. If anything, it must have been a misadventure he'd fallen headlong into and was now looking for someone to break his fall.

"What adventure?" Vikraman asked warily.

"Don't worry, it's right up your alley," Manoharan assured him. "One that involves you, me, a sayip[1] and a lion."

"Can't see the story for the narrative," Vikraman frowned.

"I've got us a sayip!" Manoharan elucidated.

"What are we going do with a sayip?"

"Hunt!"

"Hunt?"

"Yes."

'Commons' English!"

"Let me call him."

Chimban scored a penalty.

Manoharan went over to the gate and beckoned: "Sayip, come!"

The sayip came, with an army-green knapsack slung over his shoulders.

Vikraman almost got up from his chair. Sayip, the white man! The explorer of the unexplored! The colonizer of the uncolonised! The inventor of the uninvented! That supreme specimen of all things human. You want to know him, shake hands with him and befriend him. There is only one specimen that's

---

[1] Sahib. Capiche?

superior to him, the white woman. Ah, the white woman!

"I want to hunt lions," the sayip proclaimed as soon as he was presented.

That one statement and the whole story unfolded in front of Vikraman.

"Here kitty, here!" the sayip snapped his fingers at Chimban.

Chimban looked up, hissed and scooted. He didn't appear until after the sayip had left.

"Where did you find him?" Vikraman asked Manoharan in the vernacular.

"Near the waterfalls. I went ahead and said 'hello'. Couldn't help it."

Vikraman looked at the sayip. The white man. Who can help it? You yourself want to say hello. Vikraman said: "Hello".

The sayip returned the hello.

"Then?" Vikraman enquired further of Manoharan.

"He asked something to the effect of if we have lions here. If so, he wants to hunt them, and would I help him procure weapons? Honestly, I just made out the words 'lion' and 'hunt' and assumed the rest. I couldn't say 'no' to him."

Vikraman looked at the sayip. The white man. Who can say 'no' to him? Vikraman almost said 'yes.' Almost. But caught himself in the nick of time, overpowered the urge and said: "no."

The sayip looked perplexed. "No?" He was not used to the word from the natives.

"There are no lions round these parts," Vikraman explained. "Only tigers."

"Tigers!" the sayip exclaimed. He seemed thrilled.

"Yes, spotted ones," Vikraman said placidly.

"Spotted? Oh, you mean leopards! Spots would do just fine."

"All OK, then! Shake hands," Manoharan chortled and shook the sayip's hand.

The sayip beamed and shook hands with Manoharan. "All OK," he grinned and looked expectantly at Vikraman.

"Not OK," Vikraman said simply.

"What's that?" the sayip asked, confused.

"Too risky," Vikraman said.

'You've got a rifle, haven't you? He says you have a rifle!" the sayip said, jabbing his thumb at Manoharan.

"It's not about guns. In a pinch I can kill with my bare hands," Vikraman boasted.

The sayip shrugged. One can never tell with the natives. "So… what gives?"

"If caught, my youth doing porridge gives," Vikraman replied.

The sayip frowned. "He told me you are a big game hunter," he said, pointing an accusatory finger at Manoharan.

"I didn't," Manoharan defended himself quickly.

"Not in so many words. But he gesticulated to that effect," the sayip fought back.

Vikraman stuck his lower lip out as if to say, 'be that as it may'.

The sayip threw his hands up in exasperation. "Is this what you got me here for?" he turned to Manoharan angrily.

Manoharan looked at Vikraman.

The sayip shook his head and turned on his

heel. "I should have known," he muttered. Then stopped, turned around and said as though throwing his last card desperately on the table. "I'll give you one-hundred grand for your trouble, mate! How 'bout that?"

Manoharan whistled. One-hundred grand! He shot a look at Vikraman.

"You're a pushy customer, Sayvan," Vikraman relented.

"Hah, I knew it!" Sayvan aka the sayip snapped his fingers triumphantly. "And there's a lesson right there for me. One must always let money do the talking."

"While we are on the subject, might I suggest you let it sing next time?" Vikraman said. "Sing to the tune of… you know…"

"Ha! yes," Sayvan dug into his bag for the dough but frowned. "Shucks, I don't have enough," he muttered.

Vikraman looked away, stifled a yawn and called inside, "meow".

The sayip deliberated for a second and said: "I'll pay you half in cash and half in hash. How 'bout that?"

Vikraman stroked his chin. "Well, we've come this far! What can I say…?"

"Say it's a deal!" the sayip stuck his hand out.

"Deal. But cash up front."

"All right. Here you go." The sayip handed over the cash and shook Vikraman's hand. "I didn't get your name," he said.

"Vikraman, got it?"

"Wickerman?"

"No, no. Vik-ra-man."

"Wick-er-man?"

"Yeah, you got it!"

"Wickerman! All right. I'm Skinner."

"And I'm Manoharan," Manoharan interjected.

"What's that?" Skinner asked.

"Man-o-ha-ran."

"Man O'Hara? Say, that's a lot of tan for an Irish man! Ha, ha!" Skinner laughed.

Vikraman smiled - there was nothing else to do - and Manoharan produced a single but emphatic "ha!" It was the least he could do for a joke that went over his head.

Once Skinner wiped the corners of his eyes, Vikraman send him off saying, "in two days' time."

Then as Skinner toddled off, Vikraman looked at Manoharan and asked: "Now what do we do for a leopard?"

II

The next day Vikraman, Manoharan and a lamb explored the nearby hills which were said to have an 'other side'. The other side was woods, dark and deep, which were rumoured to have a big cat, the exact pattern of whose skin was not known although it was generally assumed to be spotted.

"What's the lamb for?" Manoharan asked. "Protection? In case the leopard takes a fancy to us?"

"*Au contraire*, in case the leopard doesn't take a fancy to us," Vikraman replied.

"Layman's."

"He's the bait. We tie him up and come back tomorrow. If he's gone, then we inspect the crime scene and draw our own conclusions."

"But how do we know there is a leopard?"

'That's why we are looking for the spoor."

"Are we?"

'Weren't you?" Vikraman frowned.

"Er… Of course! But what if we don't find any spoor?"

"Then we tie up the lamb and come back tomorrow. If he's gone, then we inspect the crime scene and draw our own conclusions."

"Which brings me back to my original question: how do we know there is a leopard?"

"Which brings me back to my original answer. That's what the lamb is for. You see leopards are big on lambs. Warm the cockles of their hearts."

"I thought wolves are big on lambs."

"You thought wrong. Wolves are big on sheep. Besides, lambs are rather habit-forming. A whiff and the leopard will open its eyes."

'Again, what if there isn't a leopard?"

"Then we tell Skinner that the leopards have all left the woods as part of seasonal migration and that they would be back only next year."

Manoharan asked no more questions and Vikraman answered none. The duo and the lamb trudged up the shrubby, rocky climb and soon reached the top. On the other side lay the other side where physical phenomena like light and heat seemed stuck in a black hole.

"What now?" Manoharan asked.

"Now we tie up the lamb and leave." Vikraman tied the lamb to a bush and straightened up.

'Say, here's a thought," Manoharan said. "What if the leopard has already gotten the whiff and comes now?"

Vikraman stroked his chin. "Well it's a thought."

"Speak of the devil," came a low but distinct growl from behind them.

Vikraman and Manoharan whirled around. And sure enough, advancing towards them with smouldering, fluorescent yellow eyes, was *the* leopard.

Vikraman, Manoharan and the lamb gulped.

"Well, well, well, what have we got here? Trespassers! Dishonoring the unwritten covenant," the leopard said ominously.

"What - what covenant?" Vikraman asked uncomprehendingly.

"The age-old covenant."

"What age-old covenant?"

"I'll give you a gist. Know all men by these presents: ye the villagers, ye keep away from the woods and we the tigers - spotted, striped and black - we will keep away from clearings with funny structures."

"What funny structures?"

"We believe you call them houses."

'I've never heard of any such covenant!"

"Like I said, age-old."

"Who drew it up?"

"Like I said, unwritten."

'If it's unwritten, how can it exist?"

The leopard shrugged. "*Eppur si esiste*. It exists, all the same. What are you boys up to, anyhow?" it asked regarding the duo suspiciously.

"Oh, we?" Vikraman asked.

"*Oui.*"

"Oh, we were just…," Vikraman let it trail.

"Yeah, we were just…" Manoharan echoed.

"Yes…?"

"Just… you know…," Vikraman explained.

"You know…" Manoharan echoed.

"No, I don't," the leopard growled.

"The mountain air! Yes sir, the mountain air," Vikraman replied with a snatching gesture. "On doctor's orders."

"That so?"

"That so."

"Then what's the lamb doing all tied up and looking like mutton?" the leopard asked studying the lamb.

"Oh, the lamb?"

"Yes, the lamb!"

"Why, the mountain air is for him!" Vikraman replied. "He's having a bit of trouble with his…"

"With his…" Manoharan echoed.

"With his?"

"Er… you know…" Vikraman let it trail.

"You know…" Manoharan echoed.

"No," the leopard growled.

"*Membrum virile*!" Vikraman said. "Yes, sir, the *membrum virile*!"

The leopard sneered. Humans! Always the same old shtick. How about the larynx? Or the pituitary gland? No. *Membrum virile*! It's always the *membrum virile* with them. It shook its head, took a step forward and snarled: "You lie, kid! Sold your soul to the devil, didn't you?"

"What devil?" Vikraman asked nervously.

"The white man! Always hunting us down with his barking irons to decorate his living room and for a bloody photograph. And you and your Rajas serve him your own tigers. If there's anything that reeks of the brown man's submissiveness, it's this! We don't mind giving our lives for the Rajas. Heck, we love a good hunt just as much as the next guy. But them sayips!"

Vikraman bit his lips contritely.

The leopard continued. "That's why we have to talk about The Great Bath and Dancing Girl to convince the world that this is indeed a land of great people."

Vikraman cast his eyes down and Manoharan and the lamb followed suit.

"Now get out of here before I make mincemeat out of the lot of you," the leopard snarled, throwing an involuntary glance at the lamb.

Vikraman quietly undid the rope from the bush and motioned Manoharan to follow. But they hadn't taken a few paces when the leopard growled: "Stop!"

The trio stopped.

"Turn around."

The trio turned around.

The leopard appraised the trio with a critical eye, especially the lamb, and asked: "What was the deal anyhow?"

Vikraman nudged Manoharan. Manoharan nudged the lamb and the lamb nudged Vikraman.

So Vikraman replied: "A hundred grand for a shot at you!" He came clean. He was on the needles of compunction.

"A hundred grand! For a shot at me?" The leopard seemed impressed. "Is that the going rate these days? A hundred grand?"

The trio made no answer. One can't be too sure with leopards.

With a scornful shake of its head, the leopard turned away. It climbed on a rock, raised its head and took a whiff before sweeping the woods down with its keen eyes. There was a reflective pause. Then it looked over its shoulder and said: "Very well!"

Vikraman cocked an eyebrow.

"He can have his shot," the leopard said, "and you boys, your grand."

Vikraman, Manoharan and the lamb exchanged puzzled glances.

"Provided…"

"Provided?" Vikraman asked tentatively.

"I get a cut, of course!"

Vikraman made no answer. It was the kind of situation where one hardly knew what to say.

"You boys need time to think it over, go right ahead and think it over. I'll be around," the leopard said and turned around as if to leave.

"That won't be nessy," Vikraman said quickly.

"No?"

"No."

"Well?"

"A flock of sheep," Vikraman said instinctively.

The leopard arched an eyebrow.

"A flock of sheep. Compliments of Messrs V, M & L," Vikraman said with a 'how 'bout that?' smile.

"How many?"

"Count 'em till you fall asleep."

The leopard grinned. "Aren't you just the boy for this misadventure?"

Vikraman grinned wickedly.

"You double-dealing hyena!"

Vikraman threw his head back and laughed.

"All right now, let's get down to business," the leopard said climbing down the rock. "You two," it said addressing Vikraman and Manoharan, "be bright-eyed and bushy-tailed."

Vikraman and Manoharan did so.

"Here's the plan. Let's get this over with as soon as we can. So, I suggest tomorrow. You!" the leopard pointed its right forepaw at Vikraman, "start around afternoon with Whitey but without your friend here. He is to leave separately and station himself down the hills over that precipice. Meantime you get up here with Whitey, tie up the bait and lie in wait behind those rocks over there."

Vikraman glanced at the spot.

"It's a good cover and a great spot for taking a pot-shot," the leopard continued. "I make my entrance and go for the bait. Whitey fires. Of course, the iron won't have any bite in it. Just the bark. But blood will spatter. Arrange for some Kensington. I fall dead. Your friend here gives a false alarm - maybe a whistle. Hoot! Hoot! You yank Whitey screaming 'foresters!' 'foresters!' and scram. End of story. Epilogue: a flock of sheep."

"Swell," Vikraman said, impressed.

"Well, tomorrow then," the leopard said with a wink.

"Tomorrow," Vikraman echoed, extending his hand.

"I wouldn't advise that," the leopard said.

Vikraman pulled his hand back quickly and the trio turned away with a parting nod.

"Er… one moment please," the leopard called from behind.

"Yes," Vikraman and Manoharan turned around. The lamb didn't.

"That lamb… you wouldn't have much use for it now, would you?"

III

"What, the leopard agreed to be shot at? Ha ha ha. That's rich! You guys are really witty. What? He actually did? Har, har, har. You guys are a riot. The best since… since… well, the previous best."

"So, when do we do it? Today! Even better. I like you fellas. Right after my own heart. Here, help yourself to some beer. No? What? Oh teetotaler? What? Ah! Oh, so you do. Just the local brew, is it? What's that? *Kallu*? Oh, toddy!"

"Beg your pardon? Outside your house? At Four? I can make it. All right. Toodles."

It was the next day and around two in the afternoon. Vikraman and Manoharan stepped out of the town bar where Skinner had been staying with bottles of beer and fried beef.

Vikraman looked up at the sky. The day was turning out to be just as fine as the morning had promised.

After buying a goat's bladder, adhesive and fake blood, Vikraman dispatched Manoharan to the leopard to help the latter prepare for his role. Himself, he dispatched to the market for a new lamb. That done, he went home, lunched, paced the floor and took the rifle off the wall; dismantled it, cleaned it, loaded it with blanks and waited.

At around four, Skinner appeared like clockwork with his army-green knapsack and the duo struck out towards the hills with the new lamb.

Skinner wanted to fire a few rounds, test the weapon and expressed the desire thereof.

Vikraman thought it a bad idea and expressed the inadvisability thereof. "Even the faintest rustle among the leaves here echoes in the hills. It's some kind of a natural phenomenon. Imagine what gun shots can do."

Skinner shrugged. OK.

"Where's O'Hara?" he asked after a space.

"Reconnoitering. Keeping an eye out for the foresters," Vikraman replied.

"Oh, good!" Skinner nodded his approval.

The hills were an hour's walk. The duo and the lamb crossed the coconut groves, swung over an occasional mud wall, dropped down to the low-lying grounds, squelched through the paddy fields and soon found themselves at the foot of the hills.

At which point, Skinner stopped to appraise the shrubby terrain. "Where's the lookout point?" he asked.

"It's on the west," Vikraman replied. "O'Hara must be somewhere over there," he said pointing his finger in the direction.

Skinner nodded thoughtfully.

"Let's get on," Vikraman said and started to climb up.

After throwing another thoughtful glance around, Skinner followed him up and a quarter of an hour later they finally reached the spot.

"See that?" Vikraman asked pointing towards a skeleton.

Skinner followed the finger.

"He was a lamb yesterday," Vikraman explained. "Polished him off in one sitting."

"Sups well, eh?"

"Yes, but tonight will be his last supper," Vikraman said with a wink.

"Leopardo's last supper," Skinner quipped.

Vikraman smiled. Then narrowed his eyes and looked up with a grave air. "The wind's in our favour," he concluded at length. "But we gotta make ourselves scarce. Lamb odour with human odour has a strong top note. It's called trouble."

"All right," Skinner laughed.

Vikraman knelt down to tie up the lamb.

"You are a fine man, Wickerman," Skinner said appreciatively.

"Rounds these parts, yeah," Vikraman replied with a Hollywood grimace and got up. "Let's wait behind those rocks. It's a good emplacement," he said jerking his head towards the spot suggested by the leopard.

Skinner climbed to the top of the rocks and looked around, nodded to himself and dropped down behind the lot. He lit a cigarette and eased back while Vikraman pulled out a stalk of grass and chewed on it.

Presently, the sun turned a deep orange and began to slide down along the horizon. Darkness lay in wait. The duo kept their eyes peeled and waited.

Then just as the sun paused behind the hills in its refulgent redness, a silhouette formed against it. The leopard!

Vikraman thought he heard a booming drumbeat. Like a Morricone western. It was his heart.

With its smooth golden back glowing in the evening sun, the leopard advanced like one of those dark[2], brooding, loner and misunderstood-by-the-characters-but-understood-by-the-audience-and-soon-to-be-betrayed sort of a hero.

Now there was a strange wailing effect thrown into the Morricone beat. It was the lamb.

"Leopard, leopard burning bright! In the forests of the night!" Skinner's eyes popped. "Gimme the gun, mate!" he whispered.

"Er… aren't we forgetting something?" Vikraman whispered back.

"What?"

"Your end of the bargain. The hash?"

"What? Oh god! Come on, man. Is this the time?"

'It's in your bag. Just hand it over," Vikraman shrugged.

Skinner shook his head, dug his hand in and handed it over as Vikraman gave him the gun.

Skinner took hold of the gun and held it firmly in his hands and took aim.

Vikraman took a whiff of the hash and

---

[2] In this case, spotted. Panthers are dark.

wondered what the hell he was going to do with it. Sell it back to Skinner, maybe!

The leopard paused before the lamb and let out a growl.

"Perfect!" Skinner muttered and pulled the trigger.

"Crack!" went the gun and down went the leopard, legs up.

"Tally ho!" Skinner cried and got up. "Yoohoo, I got him! Right in the belly. Ha ha."

Vikraman affected a 'yippee' and glanced expectantly in the direction of the precipice. The shot was supposed to be the cue. And right on cue, came the hoots, produced at a low frequency to simulate distance: 'Hoot!' 'Hoot!'

"Darn! the foresters!" Vikraman cried and grabbed Skinner's hand. "Let's scram!"

But Skinner wrenched his hand free.

"The foresters, they'd be here any minute," Vikraman was beside himself with fear.

"Nah!" Skinner replied coolly. "I had a good look at the terrain. It would take them at least forty minutes to get up here in this light. Plenty of time to get the job done. Or at least most of it."

"The job! What job?" Vikraman asked, bewildered.

"You think I'd spend a hundred grand just to shoot and scram?" Skinner asked with an evil grin.

"What the hell else did you want?" Vikraman asked with that sinking feeling.

"The skin, you silly, the blooming skin!" Skinner replied and fished out a skinning knife from his knapsack.

"The skin…!" Vikraman whispered and stood thunderstruck. "You're not - you're not gonna skin him!"

"No?" Skinner asked teasingly.

"But - that was not part of the deal," Vikraman protested.

"Doesn't make it any eviller, the way I see it," Skinner shrugged. "Look at it this way. We're just removing evidence. How 'bout that?"

Vikraman had no more words.

"By the way, Skinner's the trade name," Skinner winked and advanced towards the quiescent leopard.

The hoots pierced the air a few more times and died down. Seconds later Manoharan crashed out of the bushes screaming "foresters!" But it took even him only a second to discern the situation. His cry of alarm came out like a whisper.

Skinner was knelt down beside the leopard, the knife cold and white in the gloaming.

The leopard lay sideways. Skinner turned it over and brought the knife down. But no sooner had the cold of the knife touched its belly than the leopard opened its eyes and sprang up.

"What the…!" Skinner fell back with a start. But before he could finish the sentence, the claws flicked out and the paw came down in one fell swoop and struck Skinner across his throat.

Skinner fell dead.

Vikraman stuck his hand in his mouth to stop himself from screaming. Manoharan fainted.

The leopard let out a roar. Then with a deep throaty growl and smouldering eyes, it turned towards a white and trembling Vikraman.

"Help!" Vikraman cried.

The next instant the leopard was in front of

Vikraman. Raising itself up on its hind legs, it pressed its bloodied claw against Vikraman's throat and snarled: "If I ever set my eyes on you two again, I'll throw you to the wolves, chase them away and feed on you myself! Is that clear?"

"Like water," Vikraman whispered.

"Then get your friend and scram!"

"But… but… the body?" Vikraman stammered.

"What body?" The leopard asked and trotted towards what once was a sayip.

A WRESTLING MATCH
(AS A MATTER OF FACT, TWO!)

Puthukkaav 'The Bear' Raghavan is about to slam Koprakkalam 'Iron' Hydrose. It's at this climactic moment that the story begins. The next instant, Raghavan capped the climax and finished the story sending the sea of spectators into raptures.

Appu Aashaan, the referee, raised Raghavan's hand and proclaimed him the winner.

The sea surged and broke. A few hands shot out of the sea like waves and patted the champion's back.

Raghavan circled the pit acknowledging the cheers.

It was the first time in Manakulangara's humble-but-ready-to-rumble history that a wrestling match had been staged and the crowd lapped it all up.

Vikraman was also part of the spumy sea but like a whitecap that refused to break. He was too awestruck to do that.

"Boy, what a slam!" he exclaimed to no one in particular. "Boy, what a feat! Boy, what a spectacle!"

He gazed at Raghavan. The champ was not done with milking the crowd. He thumped his chest and roared: "Who's next?"

The crowd went wild and Vikraman was seized with another bout of awe. He envisioned himself in Raghavan's place; standing in the middle of the ring and acknowledging the cheers after just another day at the office. With his looks, he could be a bigger sensation. "The girls… oh! won't they simply swoon over him?"

Goosebumps.

Vikraman beamed and looked around.

That was when he realized that something had gone terribly wrong. At that moment when he had lost himself in that beautiful fantasy, some kind of conspiracy had been hatched. For the crowd was staring at him in wonder. They were no longer the raging sea. They were a silent sea.

The next instant it swelled up and broke. "Yaaaaay!"

Vikraman was confounded. Why were they cheering for him?

On an impulse, he glanced towards the pit.

'The Bear' was looking at him like his namesake with a sore head.

"What the blazes!" Vikraman exclaimed and looked around.

That's when it struck him - realization. It didn't dawn on him; it didn't shine on him but struck him like a thunderous clap of lightning.

Above the surging sea, ramrod straight, towered his right hand.

He was next!

II

Vikraman gave a start and tried to pull his hand down. Too late! The crowd was simply uncontrollable by then.

With a wide mouth and horrified eyes, Vikraman looked at Raghavan. The man wasn't dubbed 'the Bear' for nothing. He stood six-foot-two with a torso, the girth of a barrel. The muscles were not of the rippling order but were firm and taut. All he needed was hair all over his body to pass himself off as an actual bear. 'Maybe he had it shaved off for the match,' Vikraman surmised. But the beard was in place and was enough to draw parallels and drive the point home.

Raghavan slapped his arms and thighs and grinned like a butcher.

A shiver rode down Vikraman's spine. He quickly flashed a disarming and held up his palm in defense as if to say: 'Hey, just fooling around. No one's next. You're the best. Enjoy the rest ... of the afternoon.'

But Raghavan shook his head sadistically and beckoned Vikraman with his two hands.

The next instant Vikraman rose into the air, traversed the ring of spectators and alighted inside the pit[3].

Then somebody - surely, another well-meaning fellow countryman - helped Vikraman divest himself of his shirt and trousers, stripping him down to his blue briefs. Sundry hands anointed his body and withdrew.

Appu Aashaan, the referee, stood at the centre of the pit flanked by a skinny lad of some twenty

---

[3] Essentially, the crowd had lost its patience prompting an enterprising section of its to lift Vikraman up and place him inside the pit.

summers and a savage beast whose bruised ego refused to look at the turn of events as a harmless joke. He introduced the contestants. "To my left, in red briefs, the reigning and defending Heavyweight Champion of Manakulangara, 'The Bear' Rrrrrrrrrrr-aghavan!"

Applause and whistles.

"And to my right, in er" – the referee swept his eyes down – "er… blue briefs, the challenger, Vvvvvvvvvvv-ikraman."

The crowd roared its support for the Young Turk, then commended his soul to the gods.

The bell rang. The referee stepped back. The contest was on. The opponents circled the pit; Vikraman in a bid to evade Raghavan and Raghavan in a bid to catch Vikraman.

But Vikraman couldn't remain on the lam for long. With a sudden movement, Raghavan locked Vikraman in a bear hug and took the wind out of him, tossed him up and held him above his head and circled the pit with a wanton smile.

The crowd bellowed. They spared no thought for the fact that Raghavan was preparing to slam their fellow country lad and that the lad may not ever get up from that and that they may have to explain the whole thing to his kin. They were coming off the first ever wrestling contest in the humble-but-ready-to-rumble history of their village and it had only served to merely whet their appetite, not satisfy. They wanted more. They were a hungry sea. They ebbed and flowed, urging Raghavan.

Raghavan spun Vikraman around. But Vikraman didn't scream or plead for mercy. Must have been pride, something to do with 'death before dishonour' kind of stuff. But his eyes screamed blue murder!

He stared at the sea whose waves were breaking against the pit; a sea having a Roman holiday. There, at the edge of the horizon, is that ... is that, Yama? Nodding his head slowly with a crooked smile? Making a slitting motion across his neck? Pointing his crooked finger at him vengefully[4]?

Raghavan prepared to slam Vikraman.

The crowd sucked its collective breath in and held it in anticipation.

---

[4] See 'The Last Ride'.

That one moment!

The next moment the smile was wiped off Raghavan's face. For Vikraman had slid out of his hands miraculously. He dropped right behind the human bear, brought his shoulder down and swept Raghavan off his feet, leaving the wrestler with no alternative but to fall flat on his back; effectively a slam!

Raghavan lay on his back in the centre of the pit, shell-shocked.

Vikraman had done it!

But the crowd didn't scream. The crowd didn't roar. No, the crowd didn't do anything of that kind. It simply froze!

Nature froze.

Life came to a standstill. Earth stopped in its tracks and came to a screeching halt. Far away, Mars curved in and headed straight for the blue planet.

Appu Aashaan, the referee, seemed to be the only one capable of any movement. But even that was restricted to a mere oscillation. Like that of a clockwork doll, his head cut an arc between the skinny lad in blue briefs standing tall and the gargantuan figure lying supine on the soil.

It was a delicate situation, one that had the makings of an apocalypse. Luckily for the world, Vikraman was at hand.

He thumped his chest and roared: "Who's next?"

The crowd sensed a movement working up from its belly towards the throat. Life resumed. Nature thawed. Earth slowly picked up and soon cut loose. Mars missed Earth by 3.03 light minutes.

The sea, that the spectators were, swelled again. With a shout, it rose up and crashed over Vikraman, tossed him up and carried him on its crest.

Howls, shouts and whistles rang out.

"Ladies and gentlemen…," the referee made an attempt to formalize matters when a falsetto of "foul! foul! foul!" threw the celebration into *silenzio*.

The first impulse was to look at Raghavan and the impulse won. But Raghavan himself was wondering where the allegation was coming from.

So, everyone turned his gaze and traced the source. 'Iron' Hydrose! The former vanquished was shaking with indignation. "That was fixed! That was fixed! I saw the kid whispering in the Bear's ears. They were conspiring," he foamed at the mouth.

"Just what the hell do you mean by that?" Vikraman smouldered from atop the shoulders that bore him.

"Oh, you know what I mean, all right!" Hydrose spat.

"All I know is somebody is having a tough time licking his wounds," Vikraman sniggered.

"Watch it kid! You haven't bought me yet!" Hydrose warned.

Vikraman slid down, took a step forward and snarled: "Somebody, hold me back!"

Nobody did. It was all turning out to be even better than what they had bargained for. They wanted more. So Vikraman held himself back.

But Hydrose didn't. He raged. "Didn't you just challenge the world, 'who's next?' Well, *I'm* next! If you can slam 'the Bear', then you can very well slam me!"

Vikraman clenched his fist and gnashed his teeth. But left it at that.

But the crowd didn't. They clamoured: "Vikraman! Vikraman! Vikraman!"

Hydrose squared up to Vikraman.

Vikraman raised his hands. The crowd fell silent. He took a step forward, looked Hydrose squarely in the eye and proclaimed proudly: "Same place, same time in fifteen days!" Then with a cocky smile, he turned on his heel and walked away with provisional immortality.

That night, ten crisp five-hundred-rupee notes were shelled out by Vikraman to pay off 'The Bear' Raghavan.

III

The next day, *The Manakulangara Matin* registered record sales in its brief history selling twenty times more copies.

Vikraman's prodigious feat was, but naturally, the front page of the single sheet broadsheet. SLAM DUNK IN SCHOOLGROUND! screamed the headline. And under it, a hold-by-hold account by their sports correspondent.

Right next to it, another headline screamed: 'THE MATCH WAS FIXED!' ALLEGES HYDROSE. That was followed by Hydrose's allegation and the drama that unfolded.

Other interesting columns had also sprouted overnight: 'YOU TOO CAN SLAM!' a special series by Appu Aashaan and 'VIKRAMAN: WUNDERKIND OR CHINLESS WONDER?' an investigative feature. There was even an advertisement of the local gym!

The Karipankulangara Clarion, the single sheet broadsheet of the nearby village, Karipankulangara too sold an equally staggering number. MAYHEM IN MANAKULANGARA! was the screamer. They even went ahead and printed a special Manakulangara edition, effectively setting off a fifteen-day broadsheet broadside.

Sitting in a deckchair on the porch of his house, Vikraman ate it all up like a ravenous wolf. He held both rags in front of him and chortled.

"You have become an overnight sensation, my boy, an overnight sensation," he adulated himself. "Mr. Front-page. Hah!"

At that point, came the paparazzi; Printer Pappan, proprietor-cum-correspondent-cum-editor-cum-sports correspondent-cum-war correspondent of *The Manakulangara Matin* and Printer Damu, proprietor-cum-correspondent-cum-editor-cum-sports correspondent-cum-war correspondent of *The Karipankulangara Clarion*. They wanted an interview of the new sensation. An exclusive!

The sensation asked how two papers can carry the same exclusive.

They said it's all about the spin one puts on it. Besides, the readership is different. So, no one would be any the wiser.

"Maybe you should call them inclusives," Vikraman suggested. He was in a position to suggest.

"You said it!" cried one.

"Took the words out of my mouth," cried the other.

Vikraman looked at his watch with a self-important air and said: "All right, but just ten minutes, boys. Got a gym to re-inaugurate. Of course, you understand!"

Of course, the reporters were all understanding. They needed just five minutes. It was for a feature. And features are five percent fact and ninety-five percent fiction.

"Ok, fire away."

They fired.

"Did you really slam 'the Bear'?"

"Step inside the pit and ask that to my face!"

"You don't seem to have any background in wrestling!"

"Think child prodigy."

"The secret behind your superhuman strength?"

"Secret origins."

"Your response to Hydrose's allegations?"

"Pitside in 14 days…"

"What if Hydrose slams you?"

"*Avec des si et des mais, on mettrait paris en bouteille!*"

"Translate (for the benefit of our readers)."

"With ifs and buts, you can put Paris in your butt!"

Ultimately, the interview lasted half an hour. The journos thanked Vikraman and rushed back with their inclusives.

As soon as they left, Vikraman was bitten by reality. The question curved itself and straightened. "What if, indeed?"

The brow was troubled, and the chin was

stubbled. Vikraman wrinkled the former, stroked the latter and sat for '*The Portrait of a Troubled Young Man*'.

That afternoon as Vikraman stretched out on his bed after lunch, he had a dream. Hydrose had him hoisted above his head. A sadistic smile stretched his mouth. The crowd, as usual, was in raptures.

At the edge of the horizon, Yama nodded his head slowly with a crooked smile. He traced his thumb across his neck and pointed his crooked finger at him vengefully.

Vikraman woke up, drenched in sweat.

IV

The name Koprakkalam in Koprakkalam 'Iron' Hydrose denotes the village Koprakkalam that nestles - as hamlets are prone to - some three kilometers south-east of Manakulangara.

The resident wrestler had just finished his three-course dinner of mutton biryani, mutton biryani and mutton biryani and was pacing the front yard when he sensed a figure in the dark.

He stopped and growled: "Who?"

The figure stepped out of the dark and

presented itself. It wore a crumpled non-descript shirt and a white shawl around its head; the quintessential garb preferred by the countryman for undercover operations like toddy shop, bawdy house or the moonlight flit. Only the mouth was visible under the shawl and it widened in a conciliatory smile.

Hydrose regarded the figure with disgust.

"Mmm?" he asked.

"*Tête-à-tête*," Vikraman replied.

"Mmm," Hydrose grunted. Then called inside: "Shafiha, bring two chairs!"

The chairs came, one after the other, borne by a girl of about seventeen. There was an air about her that was typical of daughters with doting fathers and seemed to tell on the good heart that Hydrose was in possession of although not a bit of it was evident at that moment.

The girl brought the first chair and placed it next to Vikraman. Then went for the second.

As she passed, she smiled at Vikraman with familiarity and mischief. A smile is a smile whatever the circumstance and the susceptible young man couldn't help wonder if -

"Sit!" Hydrose jerked his head towards the chair and growled.

Vikraman sat down while Hydrose studied him with apparent distaste.

The girl reappeared with the second chair, placed it next to Hydrose and stood behind it.

"Aren't you the one who slammed 'the Bear'?" she asked with a playful smile.

Vikraman grinned sheepishly.

"Are you going to slam vapa[5] too?"

Vikraman squirmed in his chair.

"Inside!" Hydrose snapped at the girl.

But the girl was in no mood to leave off. "Can I get an autograph?" she asked.

"Shafiha!"

"Oh!" She turned away looking cross.

"Daughter?" Vikraman enquired congenially of Hydrose.

Hydrose said nothing. He folded his arms across his chest and waited.

Vikraman loosened the shawl.

---

[5] Just like Papa!

"No, let it be!" Hydrose said. "Your mug is better off covered."

Vikraman smiled and loosened it anyway. Shawls come in the way of making sorry faces.

He looked at Hydrose. Hydrose returned the look. But, said nothing. The ball was in Vikraman's court!

Vikraman looked around as though admiring the grounds.

Hydrose waited, his face slowly clouding over.

Before it thundered, Vikraman said: "Five thousand!"

A laugh rang out inside the house, like the jingle of an anklet.

"You don't look half as rotten!" Hydrose said.

Vikraman produced another conciliatory smile.

"How dare you?" Hydrose bristled. "How dare you! Instead of falling at my feet and begging my forgiveness, you have the nerve to come here and attempt to buy off my pride? My integrity? My sanctity?"

"I -"

Hydrose held up his palm.

"I've been wrestling for the last twenty years. I know it's not my daily bread. Even if it were, I know neither side is buttered. But every chance I get, I set aside all my commitments, train and wrestle. Why?"

"Er … because … you … it …"

"Because that's what defines me. I have won and I have lost. In a bid to win, I have pushed boundaries, but never have I resorted to such underhanded tactics. What happened today… 'The Bear' of all people!" Hydrose shook his head. "What did you say? Same place, same time in fifteen days, eh? You spat on my face, boy! Insulted me in front of the whole world. Made me look like a fool. And now you want me to take your money and pawn my pride?" He shook his head vehemently and looked Vikraman squarely in the eye. "Next fortnight … in the pit … I'll be waiting for you!" He rose.

"Six thousand," Vikraman said quickly.

"Shafiha, the chairs!"

"Seven thousand!"

"Dammit! Don't you get it, boy?"

Vikraman sighed and stood about looking crestfallen in a bid to work up some amount of sympathy in Hydrose when he noticed a movement to his right among the bushes.

"Who's there?" Vikraman asked tensely.

No reply.

"Who's there?" Hydrose growled and moved towards the bushes.

A figure emerged from the bushes and stood grinning. Printer Pappan's ten-year old son, the investigative reporter of *The Manakulangara Matin*.

"You!" Vikraman lunged.

But the printer's son turned into a sprinter's son and sprinted.

Even in the dark, darkness spread in Vikraman's eyes.

V

The next 14 days could be leafed through the pages of The Matin and The Clarion.

BIG NEWS! VIKRAMAN OFFERS HYDROSE 7K! EXCLUSIVE! – *The Matin*

Koprakkalam: There must be something to Hydrose's allegations after all if what transpired last night is anything to go by. The sting operation conducted by your worthy watchdog caught the so-called wunderkind - or shall we finally settle for 'the chinless wonder'? - in the act of offering seven thousand Rupees to the challenger, Hydrose, for throwing the match. The incident took place outside Hydrose's house at a quarter past nine. At the time of going to press, Vikraman was not available for comment. We rang the doorbell of his house. But there was no answer.

I SAID: 'AT LEAST 7K SPECTATORS ARE TO BE EXPECTED' – *The Clarion*

Manakulangara: Even as match fixing allegations rage around him, the Champ chose to play down the whole thing. The latest victim of yellow journalism said his exact words were 'at least 7000 people are to be expected'. While speaking to The Clarion in an exclusive 'heart-to-heart' where he talked about the challenges of growing up in an anti-grappling family, the boy-wonder admitted to meeting Hydrose, but said that it was to discuss whether they should adopt the Greco-Roman style for the big spectacular. 'I've known him for a long time. I buy mutton only from his shop,' he added.

(Read our heart-to-heart with the Slam Sensation this Sunday in our special colour supplement!)

WRESTLEGATE! HYDROSE SILENT. WE TAKE IT AS CONSENT – *The Matin*

Market: When *the Matin* caught up with Hydrose outside his mutton shop, the challenger chose to remain silent. While the Ironman didn't utter a word when asked about whether Vikraman had offered him seven thousand rupees for throwing the match, he didn't deny it either. Our correspondent couldn't help noticing that his silence was more pregnant than a woman with child.

IRONGIRL DEFENDS VIKRAMAN! – *The Clarion*

Junction: When the Clarion caught up with Hydrose's daughter outside her college, the latter cleared the air about the recent allegations and affirmed that Vikraman didn't offer her father money. We wonder if the revelation doesn't show a certain broadsheet for what it really is.

VIKRAMAN DENIES MATIN INTERVIEWS – *The Matin*

CLARION IS No 1 (EVEN IN MANAKULANGARA) – *The Clarion*

VIKRAMAN TAKING SECRET LESSONS FROM THE BEAR – *The Matin*

IT'S CALLED SPARRING, DUMMY! – *The Clarion*

The watchdogs continued to be at each other's throats for the rest of the fortnight. But all that only served to add more intrigue to the whole affair.

Vikraman vs. Hydrose became the talk of the village and Vikraman the flavour of the fortnight. College girls wrote love letters to Vikraman in their blood. Vikraman wrote back in red ink. They read them and thrilled over.

But the letters were only a small consolation for the beleaguered young man. He continued to dream of Hydrose and Yama. The former continued to hold him aloft while the latter continued to nod his head slowly with a crooked smile, trace his thumb across his neck and point his crooked finger at him vengefully.

VI

Finally, the day arrived, as sure as fate.

Vikraman stood in front of the mirror and took a final look at his reflection. Reflection looked devastated.

"Just when I was getting to know you," Vikraman's voice was barely audible.

"Pull yourself together," Reflection whispered.

Vikraman did so.

They looked at each other and nodded. Then embraced and slapped each other's back.

"Death before dishonour!" Reflection said, finally.

"Oh, bug off!"

Vikraman pulled a white bathrobe - which he

had helped himself to from his uncle who in turn had helped himself to from a hotel - over his newly bought black briefs and fitted a pair of green-tinted sunglasses. "If I'm going to die, might as well cut a dash while at it," he thought.

Outside, the sea of supporters had turned the house into an isle. It was peaceful in anticipation although occasionally a wave broke. The sea wondered: "Would Vikraman take up the gauntlet? Or would he come out clutching his stomach complaining of cramps?"

Inside, Vikraman stood facing the door. Finally, he took a deep breath, flung it open and stood incandesced in the eastern rays, just for effect!

"Yaaaaay!" The Vikraman camp roared.

Vikraman suddenly went weak in the knees. But when he saw the camera - somebody had a camera - he posed with his hands on his hips. He was safe till he reached the pit.

A lamp was lit and some traditional stuff was performed. And of course, the coconut cut an arc through the air and smashed itself to smithereens.

Everyone scrambled for a piece of the kernel

and for a moment the matter at hand was forgotten. Then somebody gave Vikraman a piece and the matter at hand was suddenly remembered.

There was another shout as Vikraman reluctantly chewed it. A red garland was thrown round his neck.

"Just what a martyr needed," Vikraman thought.

Somebody hoisted the champ up on his shoulders and the procession wended its way to the school ground.

The ground was full to bursting. People had come from nearby towns and nearer-by villages. The pit had been redone and cordoned off. An aisle had been created by way of rope partition for the wrestlers to walk down from the entrance to the ring. Like with all village festivities, nobody knew who the organizers were, but somebody was lining his pockets.

Vikraman's retinue stood at the school gate, the entrance.

A voice boomed over the loudspeaker: "Ladies and gentlemen, the champion…!"

But Vikraman didn't move. "Why am I going

first?" he asked. "I'm the champ. Champs go out last."

"Well, it's reverse psychology," came the answer. "To make Hydrose look like a real threat."

"But he is a real… er nothing."

Vikraman walked down to the pit, rotating his arms and making growly faces. And the crowd simply came alive, supporters and detractors alike.

Despite his putting on a brave front, there had been doubts as to whether Vikraman would take up the gauntlet when the day of reckoning came. After all, there seemed to be some truth in all the allegations. But what do you know! The champ himself! Walking down to the pit. Live and in living dimension! They rallied round the wunderkind.

Vikraman stood in the middle of the pit and raised his hands in acknowledgement. He looked at the turnout. He saw Shafiha under her scarf. He wanted to look away. But she pressed her hand against her heart and smiled faintly. In spite of a palpitating heart, a smile sprang to Vikraman's lips and for a moment, he forgot his troubles. It was an unmistakable gesture and the susceptible young man couldn't help wonder if –

"Ladies and gentlemen," the voice boomed

over the loudspeaker again, "the challenger!" There was a sudden silence and all eyes turned to the school gate. Koprakkalam 'Iron' Hydrose!

Hydrose made his appearance the way any self-respecting wrestler would. He was all tradition with the quintessential cape over his body.

Vikraman looked at the bounding-in monster and did two push-ups.

Hydrose entered the pit and raised his arms. The cape flew off his back. The Hydrose camp roared.

He thumped his chest and walked around the pit, threw his chest out and squared up to Vikraman, effecting a telling tale of the tape.

Vikraman stood over six feet and was broad shouldered but would have been lucky if he weighed seventy kilos. On the other hand, Hydrose would have been lucky if he stood 5'9 but weighed a hundred and twenty kilos. His arms were the size of Vikraman's thighs and his thighs the size of Vikraman's torso, if not more.

With a sneer, Hydrose turned away, but not before loosing off a parting taunt: "You still have time to withdraw, kid."

The Hydrose camp roared again.

Vikraman's face was twisted with rage. His veins stood out. He gnashed his teeth, rushed forward, locked his forehead with Hydrose's and hissed: "Ten thousand!"

The Vikraman camp came unglued. They couldn't quite catch what was exchanged. But something was. And that was all that mattered. They gave a frenetic shout and expected a scuffle before the actual match.

Appu Aashaan, the referee, immediately inserted himself between the bruisers and pushed Vikraman back. He couldn't possibly have pushed Hydrose back.

The crowd was worked into a frenzy now. Somebody shouted: "Start the match!"

"Call it right down the middle, ref!" Vikraman shouted at the referee. Then went back to his corner and emptied a can of oil over himself. The Hydrose camp cried foul. The referee said it was within the rules of the game. Hydrose said nothing. And the referee wasted no time in getting the match under way.

"Ladies and Gentlemen," he began, and silence

befell[6]. "The moment that we've all been waiting for is finally upon us. In a few moments, two forces will collide and wrestle for vindication and honour."

Applause and whistles.

"Introducing first, to my left, in white langoti, the challenger, the man of a hundred holds, 'Iron!' Hyyyyyyyyyyyy-drose!"

Loud cheers.

"And to my right, in black briefs, he is the reigning, defending –"

"The Grand Design!" Vikraman bent forward and muttered philosophically. If he was going to be buried, might as well be buried with a name.

"Eh?"

"The Grand Design," Vikraman repeated.

"You sure?" Appu Aashaan frowned.

Vikraman thought about it. The referee had a point. "All right! Make that 'The Slam-Bam Kid'. Yeah, that's the one. Go for it!"

So, the referee went for it, "the reigning, defending but disputed Heavyweight Champion of

---

[6] Some say it was the feedback from the mike that did it.

Manakulangara, the 'Slam! Bam! Kid!' Vvvvvvvvvvv-ikraman!"

Louder cheers.

Vikraman raised his hands and acknowledged his supporters grimly. "Dogs! Savages! Romans! Yeah, go on cheer! Ring the death knell."

The death knell was rung! Appu Aashaan made a motion and stepped back. The match was on!

The wrestlers circled the ring. Hydrose in a bid to catch Vikraman and Vikraman in a bid to stay alive.

But the charade couldn't be continued for long.

With a sudden movement, Hydrose charged at Vikraman and locked him in a facelock. As though he foresaw what was coming, Vikraman immediately tied his arms around Hydrose's legs. A futile attempt. The grappler hooked his hands under the lad and heaved him over. The crowd 'Oh!'ed in surprise and held its breath briefly hoping for a quick reversal. Nothing of the sort. Hydrose circled around with an air of vindication, his erect hands firmly under Vikraman's arms.

The Hydrose camp egged Hydrose on. But the rest of the crowd seemed a bit underwhelmed.

Hydrose lowered his arms and brought his opponent on his bent upper back in a bid to hurl him down. But just as Hydrose prepared to execute the slam, Vikraman prodigiously wriggled out of his hands and dropped behind him.

Déjà vu! The crowd sucked its breath in and braced itself in hopeful anticipation.

Vikraman swung round instantly and brought his shoulder down right behind Hydrose's knees. Hydrose toppled and fell backwards.

Vikraman had done it again!

With a shout, the crowd engulfed the pit. The referee and the challenger were washed away in the deluge. But Vikraman was buoyed up and he soon surfed the crowd.

Somewhere in the melee, 'the Bear' bit his lips with a frown. Then a slow knowing smile spread across his face.

VII

The night was unusually calm and quiet as though the rumbling storm clouds of emotions that had been raging for a fortnight had suddenly dissipated.

Vikraman loosened the shawl.

Across him, Hydrose regarded the young man with a faint smile. Leant back in his chair, he seemed at peace with the world.

"Why did you throw the match?" Vikraman asked.

The smile widened. "How long did the festivities last?" Hydrose asked gently, ignoring the question.

"A while…," Vikraman answered matter-of-factly.

Hydrose grunted in satisfaction. "What were they talking about?"

"Why did you?" Vikraman asked again, ignoring Hydrose's question in his turn.

Hydrose sighed. He looked away reflectively. When he spoke, he spoke with a touch of longing. "That crowd… I have never seen a crowd like that in my entire life. But they weren't there for me. They were there for you. Including my daughter." Hydrose looked Vikraman straight in the eye. "When I held you above me, I thought: "This is it? All over in a second? Is this what I had been fighting for?" And then it struck me, the irony of the whole thing." Hydrose shook his head firmly but a touch wistfully. "It would have been anticlimactic, had you lost."

Vikraman said nothing for a while. The chirr of the crickets rose and filled the silence. At length, he said: "Thank you."

Hydrose smiled. A quiet smile.

Vikraman dug into his pocket and pulled out a tiny bundle.

"Oh no, no, no," Hydrose shook his head vehemently. "You are getting it all wrong, boy."

"Not a bit. It's what I was prepared to give you."

"Listen, kid -"

"I'm not carrying it back," Vikraman said firmly.

"I'm not touching it either."

"Someone undeserving might."

Hydrose sighed. "On second thoughts, maybe I should've slammed you!"

"Let me know when you need me to return the favour," Vikraman said with a wink and got up.

Hydrose laughed.

Vikraman placed the bundle in Hydrose's palm and shook his hand when all of a sudden, the moment was bathed in a blinding flash of white light.

Vikraman whirled around.

Grinning evilly at him was Printer Pappan's ten-year old son, the investigative reporter of *The Manakulangara Matin*. He held a camera in his little hands.

"You!" Vikraman lunged.

VIKRAM VETAL

The cigarette[7] smouldered dispassionately between my lips while the smoke rose up like a stripper and sashayed into the night. I gazed at it till its smooth curves dissolved into the dark.

The night was cold and had thrown a blanket of chill over me that froze my bones. It didn't help that I was wearing only a pair of black briefs.

'Deep-freeze December,' I thought with no particular emotion and stroked my five o'clock shadow. It wasn't five yet, only two, but you get the idea.

I took one last drag of the fag end and flicked the stub into the night. It traced a red smoky line and vanished.

I pulled the sash down and turned around. Urvashi lay in bed, like a dream outside of a dream, entangled in a satin sheet that did little to cover her endlessness. Her breasts rose and fell lightly like waves of sweet slumber. In the dim light, her contours were

---

[7] Statutory warning: smoking is injurious to health. No character in this book endorses smoking.

inviting. I wanted to wake her up and hear her scream my name. But she looked tired. She'd already screamed enough.

Hell, I was too tired myself! But I won't sleep. No, I won't. Not till I had a few tipple rippling inside me.

It would be another one of those sleepless nights, I thought morosely. Sipping bourbons and smoking endlessly till the glass slipped through my fingers in the wee hours of the morning.

I crossed over to the bar. I hadn't poured myself a drink when the phone buzzed. I looked at the clock. 2:10.

"Njansheel," I cursed involuntarily. 'Who else? Who else would call me at this ungodly hour?'

I crossed the room, flicked the phone open and grunted a "yeah".

"You ever sleep?" The voice at the other end ribbed. Njansheel, always playful.

"Is that the best you could think of after waking me up?" The voice at this end growled. I, never playing along.

"I thought you never slept!" his voice

shrugged.

"We'll discuss my insomnia some other night. Right now, just spill it!"

So, he spilled it. "Ever heard of Vetal?"

I tried to think. Tried. Couldn't. "Hell is that?" I asked.

"Let's just say, someone we've been after for a long time."

I said nothing. Listened.

"I'll send you the location. Just deliver him, all right?"

For all the stuff I'd done for them, they still won't level with me.

"But of course, if you are busy, I can dial other numbers." Njansheel, still playing. But the same old shtick. And I was getting tired of it all.

"Yeah, but you won't," I said dryly.

"Don't bet on it!"

"You've already done that," I said indifferently. "Wouldn't have called me otherwise!" Dammit, I *was* getting tired of it all!

He laughed.

I wanted to cut the call on his cackle right then,

right there. But then I thought better of it. At the end of the day, it was a business call.

"I'll check my account in half an hour," I said and cut the call anyway. I felt better.

I went back and forgot all about it. Didn't bother with the glass. Grabbed the bottle by its neck and upended it. It gave it to me straight. The old number 7. December thawed inside me. I lit another and left it dangling from my lips.

Five minutes later, the phone beeped. I squinted at the screen. It glared back. But told me all that I needed to know. Amount transferred.

Now I was ready to think.

"Someone we've been after, eh?" I stroked my 5.30 o' clock and brooded. "We'll see about that!"

It took me half an hour to hack into RAW's data base. They were getting smarter by the month. Last time it took me only 20 minutes.

I punched some keys on my laptop.

A green screen lit up and started to fade into yellow. Soon it will change colour and turn red. Set off alarm bells. I had exactly one minute. Make that 52 seconds.

I scrolled down. I was surprised. The dossier was full. You couldn't have added another detail. They had all the dope on him - past activities, associates, location - heck, they even knew the exact spot where he was holed up; the charnel ground.

He was just a ghoul, a grave robber. Why the hell has no one bothered to turn him in then? I wondered. The stamp across the page said DORMANT. Maybe, that's why. That or there was a missing detail. Njan wouldn't have called me otherwise.

The page was a deep orange now. I got out. 4.37 seconds.

I narrowed my eyes. I wanted to think things through. But since thinking wouldn't have gotten me anywhere, I decided not to.

I crushed the butt and stood up. Stepped into the bathroom for a splash of cold water and caught my reflection in the mirror. It wasn't a pleasant sight. Under the swept back hair that was graying at the temples and arched eyebrows, the eyes were dead and cold; the lips, thin and uninviting; the face, tired and craggy. Lines crawled across it like cracks on a wall. The aquiline was perhaps what saved it all. Perhaps.

I splashed some water on it to improve the general aspect and stepped back into my room.

My clothes lay in a crumpled heap on the floor. I slid into my blue denims and pulled a T-shirt over; pulled a muscle, winced and got up. Shrugged into my leather jacket and thought about leaving a note for Urvashi. Nah! She'd understand. It wasn't the first time. I turned off the lights and stepped out.

Outside, cold pounced on me like a kitten. The one with two legs. Endless long legs. It clawed at me. But I wasn't in the mood for it.

I stuck my forefinger and thumb in my mouth and whistled. Bhatti came to life and stood rumbling. Bhatti; an iron steed that could do zero to sixty in a fraction. I straddled him and dug spur. Bhatti screamed through the night blazing a trail right through the chill of December.

It was a long ride. But Bhatti made it short. Really short.

I left Bhatti idling outside the charnel ground. That's where RAW said I'd find him.

Hemmed in a by a low, crumbling old wall, the charnel ground lay as ominous as a sorcerer's chamber;

smoking, sputtering and sinister.

Howls and muffled screams rose from a distance at irregular intervals.

I leapt on the wall and scanned the dump.

Screeaah…!

I ducked. A bat. Right out of hell!

Teasers, I thought contemptuously.

I dropped to the ground and walked ahead. Corpses burnt within every inch of it. Where they didn't, skulls and bones lay about.

I kicked one up into my hands. "Alas, poor Yorick! But he had it coming!" I chuckled and punted the skull. Just for the heck of it.

"Tut! Tut! That was not very nice!" came a voice from above. A voice as hollow as a marrowless bone.

I looked up. Sitting on the bough of a gnarled, leafless banyan was Vetal.

The ghoul was having his dinner, which lay in the form of a half-burnt corpse placed lengthwise on the bough.

He wore no clothes. But was none the worse for it. A white matter, like fuzz, covered his short, gangling, cadaverous form. Thin long white hair emanated from his skull like swirling wisps of smoke.

He licked the grease off his fingers and put his hand out. "Vikram, I presume!" he presumed.

"Good. Formalities are over. Now get on my back," I said acidly.

"In a hurry?" he asked in mock surprise. "Won't you stay for dinner?"

I wasn't going to waste my time on any of that. With any luck I could be back home for the rest of the bottle before sunup. I pulled out my X26. Taser. Civilian Issue.

"Dinner? Why not?" I shrugged and levelled the neuromuscular incapacitator between his legs. "Eat this!" I snarled. "Compliments of Njansheel."

"Whoa, whoa, whoa, whoa!" he said quickly, drawing back and shielding his nuts. "Take it easy, now. Which one?"

"Which one what?"

"The shoulder. Left, or right?"

II

I slung him over my left shoulder and walked

back to edge of the grove where Bhatti waited. But my mind was racing. It was too easy. In a minute I'd be out of the woods. Literally and figuratively. What was the catch? Njan didn't need me for this. Any old joker would have done just fine.

"It's gonna be a long walk back home," he said as if answering my question.

"I've got a bike!" I growled.

"I mean, till we get to the bike. It's gonna be a long walk back."

I said nothing.

"So, let me tell you a story."

"Suit yourself," I said indifferently. I couldn't care less. I just wanted to get to my bike. It was parked outside the wall. But - where was the wall?

Somehow the wall seemed to have disappeared! And every step I took, a fresh stretch of land seemed to rise before me. Like in an endless running game. Only I was walking.

Vetal cleared his throat.

I sighed.

"Not a long time ago," he began, "and not very far from here, in a hamlet, there lived a Brahmin and his wife. Post the land reforms, they had lost all their holdings and were living in genteel poverty.

Since the reforms hadn't spared even the landlords, there weren't many rich households left that could afford *poojas* on a regular basis. Therefore, calls to perform rituals were few and far between.

On most days, the *naivedyam* from the temple was the only meal.

Since the Brahmin had a higher metabolism, his already spare figure spared further. But the woman enjoyed a lower met and continued to be a dish despite all this. That is just by the way.

Now, in the hamlet, there resided a youth - among other youths - a twenty something reprobate by the name of Vikatan.

Now this particular youth was often beleaguered by certain hormonal imbalances that rendered him amorous and he resorted to the age-old cure of sowing his wild oats whenever he could. Needless to say, he had designs on the dish.

Therefore, one day while the man was away on a chance business, the youth, under the pretext of calling on him, called at his house.

He maintained a respectable distance from the door - as was the custom in those days - and called: 'Tirumeni … Tirumeni … Is no one home?'

The woman, like those chaste one-timing wives of the yore, opened the door a fraction, stood behind it and enquired: 'who's there?'

'It's me, Vikatan,' the youth replied.

The woman frowned from behind the door. 'It's I, Vikatan!'

'Yes … yes, indeed. It's *I*, Vikatan and it just occurred to *I* that it's been a while since *I* have enquired after your man. Is he not here?'

'Afraid not. He's away on business, a three-day pooja.'

'Oh, that's indeed good news,' Vikatan said.

At this, the woman smiled sadly. Vikatan understood the meaning of her sad smile. With the money, maybe they could manage three squares for a week, but the wolves were bound to return soon, smacking their lips.

Now the youth had an eight-anna coin in his hand. Though decimalization has since then reduced eight-anna to a fifty-paisa coin, it used to be quite a tender in those days.

Presently, the reprobate started playing with the coin with a callous air even as he exchanged pleasantries with her.

Noticing the coin, the woman surmised: 'You must be on your way to the market.'

'Eh? Er… well, you could say that,' Vikatan replied.

The woman laughed. 'What else could be said?'

Vikatan pretended to be cornered. 'Well, er… I mean, yes, to the market. To the market, indeed,' he said and turned his head away as if he were trying to hide a naughty smile.

'Do I smell mischief?' the woman asked with a playful frown.

'No mischief. Just the indulgences of the youth,' Vikatan replied.

'Indulgences of the youth? What indulgence would that be?' the woman asked.

Vikatan pretended that he had no choice but to come clean. He looked down and owned up. 'I won't hide it from you anymore. This is for Menaka.'

'Menaka? You don't mean…!'

'Afraid so.'

'What business could Vikatan possibly have at that bawd's house?' the woman asked looking concerned.

'The very!'

'Shiva! Could this be true? Do my ears deceive me? Let Tirumeni come back. I'll ask him to talk some sense into you!'

'Oh, I can't help it!' Vikatan exclaimed looking hurt. 'You know how it is. A man can't marry until he is at least twenty-six and if he's got a sister, he can't till she has. And if there are faults in her stars, then he's a goner!'

'I'm not saying there are faults in her stars or that I even have a sister, but you get the idea. I'm barely twenty and my hormones are giving me sleepless nights.'

'And is this your solution? That woman of ill repute?'

'She does it for a living! It's better than starving oneself to death.' Here Vikatan paused to let the thought sink in. Then continued: 'And mind you, she doesn't entertain everyone. It's no dice unless you are an upper-class Nair. My uncle Shankunni even has an account.'

At this, the woman coloured a deep shade of red.

'I beg your indulgence as I describe her,' Vikatan continued. 'She sits on the *chapramancha* next to a betel-box, clad in just a one-piece *kasavumundu* that she gathers above her round breasts. She smiles at you teasingly. Then applies lime on the betel leaf rather indifferently. She spends ages on this. The whole thing is meant to make you drool like a ravenous wolf. There is a reference to this in some of the old texts like *srgalaleela*.'

'Then she invites you to sit next to her and hands you the preparation. She tells you stories of adventurers, adulteresses, sugar daddies and cougars - essentially regional Decamerons - while you indulge in a bit of fumbling. By the time you tumble, you find yourself having transformed into a subject of some kind of high-art.'

'Indeed, the whole thing is treated like a work of art. The kind that the Aryans referred to as *Sturm und Drang*. I went there a boy, came back a man,' Vikatan concluded emphasizing the last word.

The poor woman turned pale upon hearing such unabashed and graphic account of Vikatan's romp.

But all said and done and as improbable as it may sound, there is nothing like unabashed sincerity to disarm a woman. It's as though you have laid all your cards on the table. There is no ace up your sleeve. No doubt, it disconcerts her. But it gets her thinking.

'Anyway, I must be going. I'll drop by when he is back.' Saying thus, Vikatan turned around to leave.

But no sooner had he taken three paces than he heard the woman say rather impetuously: 'He'd be three days ...'

It was a piece of information that was given earlier. But upon reiteration, it assumed a new meaning. And that meaning was not lost on Vikatan. He stopped and turned around slowly.

The gap between the door and the frame was now wider. He could see the unsteady rise and fall of her right bosom under the damp white blouse.

Her face was tense, and she seemed to have trouble breathing. Her lips parted in anticipation of the necessary sin. A bead of sweat formed around her white throat. It rolled down her neck and plunged. Just for effect.

The door opened further.

Vikatan cast a quick glance around and went inside. The door closed.

There are no secrets in the countryside. When the good man returned, it didn't take him long to smell a rat. The gods whose benisons he had set aside his life to invoke were no longer powers of strange ways, but rather powers with a cruel sense of humour.

He was beside himself with grief and soon ended his life on a rope.

Thanks to a countryside that set aside its precepts when night fell, the woman soon put Menaka out of commission. That is, by the way."

"Now, tell me, Vikram, who was ultimately responsible for the man's death: the reforms that impoverished him, the wife who couldn't cope with the privations of life or the youth whose hormonal imbalances gave him sleepless nights?" Vetal asked.

I don't think I answered. I was lightly snoring by then. Yes, sleep walking, if you will. But I vaguely recall him lament - as he freed his hands from mine and scurried back to his branch - "Cor, what story shall I cook up to put him to sleep tomorrow?"

THE LAST RIDE

It was a frame straight out of Lawrence of Arabia; a man and a bike. The man was Vikraman and the bike was a 500 cc.

Vikraman straddled the bike, hitched up the sleeves of his denims, strapped the glovelettes tight, pulled the riding goggles down, started the bike, revved up the engine and shifted into first gear.

Released the clutch and crossed the gate. Into second and went as far as the first turn. Took it nice and slow and immediately moved into third. Another turn. Stayed in third. A few more turns later, he hit the main road. Moved into fourth. Took a left and hit the woods.

Here the traffic was light, the road winding and the turns nicely banked. Lefts and rights alternated the stretch. Vikraman cranked up the throttle and dived down.

Chickens cackled and flew, dogs yelped and scampered and cats crouched and hissed[8].

---

[8] The cats were otherwise nonchalant.

Vikraman cut arcs, wobbled dangerously and lived on the edge, but remained alive and largely in third gear. Finally, the turns ended, and he slowed down bringing his bike to a halt.

But he didn't cut the engine. He kept revving it up and surveyed what lay ahead of him and decided that he was indeed monarch of all he surveyed. What lay ahead of him was another stretch - flanked by paddy fields on either side.

Here the traffic was few and far between, and the road, straight and two miles long!

The tarmac lay sizzling in the heat, sending forth fumes from the melting tar. Vikraman closed his eyes and took a whiff. It fired him up.

Vroom ... vroom ... the bike strained at the brakes.

Vikraman cocked a smile, pressed his heel and released the clutch. Into second. Into third. Into fourth. Into fifth. He put his head down. The bike whizzed by.

The needle hit hundred straightaway and continued to crawl up. Around him the landscape blurred into an impressionist painting and fell away.

But two miles is not a long haul at that pace and as he neared the final hundred meters, Vikraman reduced speed. Too late! The van that came round the corner also had a lunatic behind its wheel.

A collision was inevitable. The van 'thunk'ed the bike head on and sent the ton-up kid sailing towards his fate.

The airborne Vikraman cut a wide arc and made straight for a milestone, cracked his head on it and lay dead for all intents and purposes.

The van drove off without stopping, leaving the body to be cleared up by the circling vultures[9].

Vikraman lay, a bloodied mess, too stunned to feel the pain, but aware of his evanescing consciousness. Around him blood poured out and fizzled into mists of red vapour upon touching the hot road.

His whole life flashed before his eyes; the first flash of light, the first taste of milk, the first rush of love … the last stretch that he scorched moments before and the final arc he cut in the air.

---

[9] There are no vultures where Vikraman comes from. Only crows. They double up as vultures in a pinch.

Thoughts wandered. Vision blurred. Images kaleidoscoped.

The heat haze hung low like a curtain to the other world.

Vikraman laid his head back and uttered a prayer.

Just then, a light rumble coursed through the tarmac, the kind that a chopper would make. Vikraman raised his head painfully, blinked the blood off his eyes and peered.

Like a scene straight out of a Hollywood movie, from the shimmering heat haze, there emerged a shapeless form. It appeared like a wave of hot air slowly detaching itself from the haze. Soon the shape of a man on a bike formed. It left behind the pool of mirage that washed the molten road and pulled up next to Vikraman.

'That's one hell of a chopper,' Vikraman thought in spite of himself.

One hell of a chopper indeed! It looked like a giant buffalo stripped to its bare bones riding a pair of wheels - or was at least modified to create the effect. The skull with its long spread out horns formed the headlight and the handlebar. The ribs caged in the fuel tank and the seat was the vertebrae upholstered in leather in its purest form; skinned buffalo hide!

"Only a hell of a guy can ride this beast," Vikraman concluded and looked up.

One hell of a guy indeed! And equally custom-modified. He wore a black bandana and a pair of dark shades. A horseshoe moustache curved round his lips and tapered down to the chin. The sideburns were a given. The rest of him were black boots, denims, a big belt buckle embossed with the skull of a buffalo and a black sleeveless leather jacket that he left open revealing his tattooed chest and arms. Strange mythical beings twisted around them in green and red. Round his neck was another. 'Memento Mori!' But what truly defined the man on the machine was the coil of rope that was slung round his shoulders.

"Yama," Vikraman whispered and felt his heart sink. The Grim Reaper of his mythos.

Yama pushed his shades up and revved up the engine a few times as though the sight of roadkill gave him a rush. The sound thundered into Vikraman's ears and tormented him.

At length Yama laid off, spat a swathe of tobacco juice and said: "Speed thrills, but it also kills!"

Vikraman lowered his head back and sighed. Then sputtered: "Shut the hell up and take me to a hospital, you son of a double-barrelled gun!"

"Haar, Haar, Haar…" Yama roared with laughter. It echoed like the revolutions of his chopper and seemed to go on forever. Finally, after hitting the crescendo at the forty-second mark, it diminuendoed.

"I'll give you a ride, all right, son. Soon as you're done breathing. Your last ride," he chuckled.

At that moment, the road shook as another rumble coursed through the tarmac, the kind that hits a six on the Richter scale. It came round the corner and metamorphosed into a truck.

There was a loud thud and an agonizing wail.

The next instant the truck sped towards a nearby hospital bearing Vikraman.

As the truck passed, Vikraman stuck his head out and looked. Yama's custom-modified chopper lay in a mangled heap among the paddy, smoking. But there was no sign of Yama.

EL MURCIÉLAGO

Vikraman waited, a regional *torero*.

Manikantan snorted, dust flew up.

Gounder looked on, a nail biting spectator.

Manikantan pawed the ground, soil fell away.

The farmhands clamoured, simulation began.

Manikantan charged.

Vikraman crouched.

Manikantan passed.

Vikraman lunged.

He swung his leg over the rampaging bull and clamped his right hand on its hump while his left instinctively dug into its body. The bull instantly twisted its frame and whipped its body to throw off the aggressor.

The aggressor on his part clenched his teeth and clung on like grim death. Around him, shouts and yells rose up and clattered into the thunderous explosion of the hooves under him.

The farmhands bellowed, simulating the grand annual that the whole exercise was in aid of, the Jallikattu, meaning a purse of coins tied to the horns of the rampaging bull, the snatching of which ends the contest. There is another purse at the end of the line if you can go a stipulated distance with the bull. If you can!

Lasting the bull was out of the question. Vikraman knew that. Manikantan was the wrong bull to lock horns with. He was a true *murattu kalai*, an angry bull! It was as though the chaos unsettled him, infuriated him, maddened him, till everything around him turned red.

That year's would be Manikantan's first Jallikattu and there was a lot of anticipation surrounding him. He had already made waves at the preparatory events, having run roughshod over seasoned bullfighters and the word on the street was that he was the finest and fiercest bull to have ever nailed up two pairs of shoes.

So, Vikraman set his sights on snatching the Jallikattu. Lunge, grab the Jallikattu and the bull could buck his way to kingdom come for all he cared.

He waited for the split-second trough between the violent crests of jerks and took his right hand off. It hooded over the Jallikattu for a moment before coming down on it like the sudden strike of a snake. But with one sudden violent jerk of his own, Manikantan tossed Vikraman over and bounded away.

There was a momentary lapse of din as the farmhands held their breaths in disbelief before erupting in unceremonious joy. Manikantan had done it!

Vikraman later said he spun thrice in the air, righted himself, landed on his two feet, drew to his full height, watched the bull bound away and shook his head appreciatively; a true champion acknowledging another.

But in reality, he had landed on his haunches hard and had rolled away. It was a nasty bump and he had a tough time hiding his limp as he walked back.

But Gounder who had chewed off all his nails by then wasn't so sure of the result. He searched the youth all over. Had he managed to snatch the Jallikattu before being thrown off? No, he hadn't. There was no Jallikattu in his hand! Rather, it clutched his left thigh as he limped back. Manikantan had truly done it! Gounder was all glee inside and said in an undertone: 'Serves you right, you mangy dog!'

But when Vikraman walked up, he was all concern. "You all right?"

"I'll live!" Vikraman replied with a grimace, inspecting his bruised arms and legs. "But the day he's done, I'll have his broth!" he looked over his shoulder at the now serene animal. "The devil!" he swore.

"Ha, ha, ha," Gounder laughed good-naturedly and slapped Vikraman on his back.

Vikraman shook his head and limped away.

Gounder twirled his handlebar and followed him with his eyes. He liked Vikraman, but he liked his bulls more. They were his pride and joy. And every year, they brought him glory. Gounder's bulls! With them the stakes were high! Your life! No one dared go near them during their run.

But Gounder's bulls never went out last. That distinction went to the bull that Vikraman set his sights on. For, with Vikraman involved, there was bound to be a contest. And a contest was what the crowd came to see.

Year on year, a new bull threatened to toss Vikraman. But, inexplicably, Vikraman never lost. Some put it down to *Kadathanadan Kalari*, the northern school of the southern martial art form, while some put it down to *Tulunadan Kalari*, the state-of-the-art, out-of-state school of the martial art form. In any case, he remained untossed. And that naturally prompted the question: "why can't the untossed be pitted against the tossers of Gounder?"

The fable agreed upon was that since Vikraman was the head test fighter for Gounder, it naturally put Gounder's bulls at a disadvantage.

But the Gallup poll showed that it was all bull and the general consensus was that Vikraman had more horns than the bull. That naturally irked Gounder. But now here was something. Manikantan had tossed Vikraman! The impossible had happened.

Once Vikraman was out of earshot, Gounder beckoned Silamparasan, his right-hand man and instructed: "Put the word out. I want every Murugan, Selvan and Munisami to know that Manikantan has tossed Vikraman like an *uthappa*[10]. Then they can make up their minds as to why Vikraman never goes after Gounder's bulls. See to it."

---

[10] Just like a pancake. But served with *chutney*.

"There's no need," Silamparasan replied with a smirk.

"Eh?"

"The men have already gone to town."

"Have they?"

"Yes. And they will soon be shouting from the rooftops."

"Ah! ha, ha," Gounder laughed self-indulgently.

"He's not a bad egg," Gounder remarked looking at the receding figure. "It's just that he's too darned good. But this time Manikantan's going out last."

"If he doesn't, they'd riot!"

"Aah!" Gounder stroked his moustache. Then his eyes narrowed as though a sudden thought struck him. He chewed it over momentarily and said rather meditatively: "And this time the prize just got … priceless!" He looked at Silamparasan. "An emerald necklace instead of the jallikattu!"

"An emerald necklace?" Silamparasan's eyes widened.

"No. *The* emerald necklace."

"*The* emerald necklace! You don't mean…?"

"I do! Yes, the heirloom."

Silamparasan gasped. "It would be a sight unmatched, no doubt. But…!"

"I know what you're thinking. What if? What if? And I say look at him," Gounder pointed at Manikantan. "Six-hundred kilos of *Murattu Kalai*. Didn't you just see what he did to Vikraman?"

"I want him to debut in style," Gounder continued. "The tales of his exploits must resound like the explosion of his hooves. Years from now, people must say: Pah, you call these bulls? Oh, don't you make me laugh! Just a sham. That's what they are, if you ask me. Keep the tradition going, they do. But that's all there is to them. There once was a bull by the name of Manikantan. Oh, there never was anything quite like him. He belonged to Veeramani Gounder. I still recall his debut. Gounder sent him out with an emerald necklace tied to his horns instead of the Jallikattu. Oh, it was a sight for the ages! And we all just stood there mesmerized. I tell you, there never was a sight quite like that."

Gounder stroked his handlebar. He felt a

strange sense of elation and pride, something which he had never experienced before. And his heart was pounding away quietly.

II

Meanwhile, Vikraman went home straight, washed up and sat down on his bed gingerly. His back and legs were sore. But he didn't quite mind that. It was his pride that hurt him more. It was sorer.

"Darn, if only I had been able to snatch the Jallikattu!" he thought like a revisionist historian. But he knew it couldn't have been helped. Manikantan was all that he was touted as and more. What made him dangerous was the rhythm of movement that he seemed to lack. Unless one judged quickly, one found oneself biting the dust, literally and figuratively.

He closed his eyes and lay back, rewound the spool of his memory rather involuntarily and played it. The film was in Technicolor and moved at a rate of sixteen frames per second.

He saw himself as a younger man at a Jallikattu, transfixed by the mesmerizing sight of a charging bull. The sudden spasmodic movement of its sinews, the thunderous hooves flashing through the clouds of dust, men throwing themselves upon its heaving back - a metaphor for nature and man's unending quest to conquer it. He forgot what he had come for and stayed back.

Maybe he was a natural or maybe he was an unnatural. Either way he saw himself essaying epic after epic - *Alanganallur, Palamedu, Pudukkottai* - a modern day Hector, but one who tames bulls.

He fast-forwarded the spool and played it from the morning.

He saw Manikantan on the rampage, twisting his frame and whipping his body while he held on tenaciously: every single movement, every single jerk, every single kick, the crests, the troughs, the sudden violent toss, the pratfall, the roar and the tremulous undercurrent of delight Gounder's concerned face failed to check.

The tape wound on and caught up with the present.

His back and legs were sore. But he didn't quite mind that. It was his pride that hurt him more. It was sorer.

He paused the reel and rewound it. Manikantan was on the rampage, twisting his frame and whipping his body while he held on tenaciously…

III

Jallikattu was hardly a week away and the village had come alive. At the heart of it was Manikantan, the ground-pawing, nostril-blowing, six-hundred kilos of Murattu Kalai. But what made the heart beat faster were talks of the career-ending injury he had inflicted on Vikraman and the ensuing rumour that Vikraman may have to give the event a miss.

But Vikraman denied it vehemently. He would get up proudly, make threats and limp away.

Gounder grew concerned over this and persuaded Vikraman to head back home to his folks to nurse his injury.

"Oh, don't you lose your sleep over all this talk," he said by way of bolstering up the morale of the fallen hero. "Let them talk. What else are they good for? What's that they say about the crowd? The many-headed monster! No, that's not the one. Ah, yes. That it's fickle! Just imagine the anticipation when you return next year. The kind that kills. You'd be much in demand. They'd hail you as the returning king."

Vikraman stroked his chin. A cogent argument!

"Why, you could even work a program with Manikantan! A return match. A champion vs. champion spectacular. I mean, technically you would still be undefeated. We could even collect gate!"

"The Champede!" Vikraman said instinctively.

"Now! That's the spirit." Gounder held Vikraman by his shoulders and shook him.

Vikraman nodded grudgingly, but the fine print of 'technically' to his championship status was not altogether lost on him. But for all intends and purposes, the matter seemed to have been settled.

IV

Finally, the day arrived and ushered itself in. The village and its outlying parts woke up to shouts and bellows and general display of revelry. Little snotters-in-knickers ran around holding their forefingers to their heads and blowing their nostrils[11].

---

[11] Which was not a pretty sight.

Men took bath and women strutted their stuff.

The roads welcomed the day with many-coloured ribbons and trimmings. Posters lined the walls with promises of rewards. Smiling faces of bull-owners looked on while behind them an angry bull pawed the ground.

Jallikattu began. The bulls were released from the enclosure. Valiant youth took them on. The day progressed, every passing second taking it closer to the main event.

A few hours before Manikantan's turn, Gounder arrived, to all round cheers and whistles, flashing a fine row of thirty-two and took his place in the sun.

And moments later Vikraman limped in, to all round silence.

"Did you hear that?" Gounder asked Silamparasan who was standing by his right side.

"What?"

"The crowd."

"Er... no."

'Exactly! They don't care about him anymore. He's finished. Heh heh. That's the thing about the crowd. They want a new king every time."

"And the coronation won't be long," Silamparasan reassured.

"Aah!" Gounder twirled his moustache.

Vikraman walked up.

"Wotcher?" Gounder asked.

"Notcher!" Vikraman replied looking all down and out. "I went to the doctor's yesterday. It's worse than what I had thought."

"Oh!" Gounder looked worried.

"It's a Blighty bump. He suspects that the spine maybe involved."

Gounder appeared remorseful. "It's all my fault," he muttered shaking his head. "I shouldn't have put you in his way. I should have known that Manikantan was no ordinary bull."

Vikraman winced. Insult to injury.

"Oh, well, what's done is done," Gounder threw up his hands.

"I guess it's homeward for R&R for me," Vikraman said. "I came to wish you all the best."

"What? Don't tell me you are not staying for the main event!"

"I don't have the heart. Besides, the bus leaves in half an hour," Vikraman made a face.

"Well, I won't insist," Gounder got up. "But a shame, nonetheless. We are sending him out in style."

"I heard."

"You heard, eh? *The* emerald necklace! How about that?"

"Glitzy!"

"Ha, yes! Anyway," Gounder embraced his old rival, "get well!"

"I will!"

"And don't forget 'the Champede'," Gounder winked.

"I won't," Vikraman smiled uneasily and turned away.

"Whose bull is next?" Gounder asked Silamparasan.

"Pandiyan's."

"Ah, the filler." Gounder eased back in his chair with a sense of vindication.

V

By afternoon, the mid carders were all done. Mostly the bulls won. That bode well for Gounder though he couldn't help feel a bit nervous as Silamparasan said excitedly: "Manikantan is next!"

Presently, the announcer echoed the same sentiments and anticipation muffled the crowd. Gounder slid to the edge of his seat and munched on his nails. Any moment Manikantan would storm out sending the crowd into raptures. He braced himself.

But the moment never came.

What came was a sharp neigh of a horse that startled time and shocked it to stillness and before it could recover, shattered it further with the thunderous echo of its galloping hoofs.

Everyone whirled around in wonder. But they didn't have to wonder for long. As they looked, a mounted figure charged in, cut an arc over them in a blaze of red and reared on his horse.

The crowd gasped.

A masked man!

Gounder bolted up from his seat and gawked.

A few women swooned and had to be carried away. Their men thought it was the heat. They didn't know better.

So, let's sketch the portrait of the Masked Man

with a few squiggles of the pen. He wore a black cloth mask that covered his face down till the aquiline. A twirled-up mouthbrow lined the upper lip, while a slender soul patch tapered down from under the lower. A black *chaquetilla* and black breeches embroidered in gold[12] pretty much rounded him out. He set it all off against a red cape.

The crowd looked at one another for answers. Who was he? Where did he come from? Why was he wearing a mask? Was he a bandit? Was he armed? Was he dangerous?

But they didn't have to look further. The answer emerged from within, in the form of a small dark figure jostling against them and shouting: "Make way, make way."

The crowd made way.

The small dark figure carried a stool in one hand and a gramophone in the other and took his place next to the Masked Man.

They stood there like modern day Don Quixote and Sancho Panza, ready to tilt at windmills.

---

12 The 'Suit of Lights' for the initiated.

Rocinante whinnied.

Sancho - let's call the small dark man Sancho - set the stool on the ground and placed the gramophone on top of it. He released the catch of the device and a hitherto unheard-of music blared. *España Cañí*, the pasodoble.

Upon this, the Masked Man smiled proudly and gave his man a nod.

The man nodded back.

The Masked Man nodded again.

The man nodded back again.

The Masked Man rolled his eyes and jerked his head pointedly.

At this, the man's lips rounded in an 'O' and his hand dived into his pocket. It surfaced instantly with a folded piece of paper which he proceeded to unfold. Once done, he looked at the Masked Man and nodded.

The Masked Man regarded the crowd prefatorily. Then spoke: *"¡Mi nombre es Vic Ramon Indio de España y Matador de Toros!"*

"My name, big name!" Sancho translated.

The Masked Man raised his right eyebrow

under the mask and shot the interpreter a stern look. That was not part of the plan.

Sancho shrugged helplessly. Unforeseen circumstance. Too many 'y's and 'r's.

The Masked Man nodded understandingly and continued: "*¡Pero me llaman El Murciélago!*"

"But they call me 'The Bat!'"

Gounder leant forward in his chair and whispered to Silamparasan: "*Intha maatiri oru pesum padamirukku*[13]."

"*Chorro*[14]"

"*Atu taan*[15]."

"*Yo soy un torero*," the Masked Man continued.

"I am a bullfighter," Sancho translated.

"Oh!" The crowd murmured.

"*¡Muy famoso!*"

"Very famous."

"*¡Muy muy famoso!*"

"Very, very famous."

The Masked Man glanced at his gloved hand

---

[13] 'There's a movie just like this.'
[14] 'Zorro'
[15] 'That's the one!'

and reeled off: "*Vengo de España, la verdadera tierra de las corridas de toros.*"

"I come from Spain, the true land of bullfighting."

"*Pero he oido que tienes algo más peligroso.*"

"But I hear that you have something more dangerous."

The Masked Man leapt off his horse and stood with his hands on his hips before throwing a challenging look at the crowd.

"*¿Es así?*"

"Is that so?" Sancho translated with the same amount of grit and challenge in his voice as that of the Masked Man, his arms too akimbo.

"*¡Suelte el toro!*" the Masked Man shouted.

"Rrrrr-release the bull!" Sancho shouted.

The crowd looked at one another again and murmured. But this time it was all very clear to them. The masked man wants a fight. And if he wants a fight, he'll have it! Oh, and we have just the bull for you, Mr Masked Man. Manikantan!

They looked at Gounder.

Gounder rose from his chair and fixed the

Masked Man with a cold, venomous glare. The Masked Man met his glare and stood his ground like a statue while his fluttering red cape did a hundred 'Veronicas'.

Someone started it and soon others joined in and before Gounder knew it, everyone was chanting his name.

"Gounder!" "Gounder!" "Gounder!"

With the crowd behind him, Gounder was once again his usual self. That was his day. That was Manikantan's day. And no 'son of nothing' was going to snatch it away from them. He raised his hand and motioned the crowd to silence.

He stroked his moustache, turned to Silamparasan and growled: "Let him have it!"

The crowd roared. It was deafening. Silamparasan narrowed his eyes evilly and left the stands. He didn't appear again.

But Manikantan did. He appeared blowing out his nostrils and charged out.

The Masked Man unclasped his cape and let it fly away. The wind caught it and whipped it towards the crowd and caused quite a scramble.

"*¡Olé!*" he cried.

"What was that?" the crowd asked itself.

"Something to the effect of 'olé'," the crowd answered itself.

"Olé!" the crowd echoed.

The beast charged at the Masked Man. The Masked Man sidestepped nimbly and flung himself upon the animal's back as it passed. There was a roar from the crowd as he did so. It would have been anti-climatic had he failed to do at least so much.

The rest was all the business of a split second. But since an epic cannot be told in a second, let's view it in slow motion.

Here we see the bull passing. Notice that the Masked Man is in mid-air, his hands barely touching the hump.

Here we see the bull still passing. Notice that the Masked Man is atop the bull.

Here we see the bull ready to throw its body. Notice that the Masked Man is preparing to lunge.

Here we see the bull bucking. Notice that the Masked Man is nowhere in the frame.

Here we see a cloud of dust. Notice that both the Masked Man and the bull are nowhere in the frame.

Here we see a figure emerging from the cloud of dust. Notice that it's the Masked Man and that the Masked Man is holding something aloft and that it's an emerald necklace.

The crowd erupted in real time.

They started to climb over the barricade in a bid to engulf their mysterious hero.

But the mysterious hero foresaw the danger and decided to make himself scarce.

He stuck his thumb and forefinger in his mouth and whistled.

Rocinante whinnied and galloped towards him. The next instant the Masked Man leapt on his horse and disappeared in a cloud of dust, but not before rearing on his horse one last time. For the cameras. Hiya!

The moment of truth was too much for Gounder. He stood stock-still for a space, then sat down with his hands on his head as though somebody had cracked him on the head.

VI

The Masked Man and his exploits took the little

village and its outlying parts by storm.

The identity of the Masked Man was ascertained to be uncertain but his nationality, Spanish. Women began to groom themselves to be Rosas and Estellas. The traditional handlebars were replaced by swanky mouthbrows and soul patches made occasional appearances. Little snotters ran around in cloth masks ridding the world of evil and for a while *España Cañi* threatened to drown out *Suprabhatam*.

People expected the Masked Man to make a return the next day or the next day or the next day. But the Masked Man did no such thing. He remained a mystery prompting urban legends and such. A couple of imaginative youth thought that was their chance and staged a few sightings masquerading as the Masked Man. But that came to an abrupt end after mysterious attacks befell them. One broke his arm. The other, his leg.

Meanwhile, the local children's magazines seized the moment and presented their young readers with The Vivid Adventures of the Masked Man. *The Cabal of Cannibals*, *The Trrring of Terror* et al. He saves the day.

The pulps moved in right after. 'Coming soon…!' *Never Love a Masked Man*, *Confessions of the Masked Man*, vivider adventures of the Masked Man. He gets the girl. And her sisters.

A B-grade movie was also advertised.

By the time Vikraman returned, the brouhaha over the Masked Man had abated although he continued to cut a dash across the innumerable pages of *Ana Dreadfuls*. The mouthbrows were thickening and once again *Suprabhatam* was the most requested song.

When Vikraman went to Gounder's house, the latter wasn't home. So, he went to the local newsagent's and picked up the latest offering from *The Masked Fantasy* that was topping the best sellers list; *The Masked Man and the Volatile Virgin!*

It was an unputdownable. Vikraman plonked down on his bed and devoured it. Time flew. Darkness descended.

Just when Sheela's sari slid off her shoulder quite accidentally while the Masked Man was in a compromising position, a knock came on the door.

"The devil take it!" Vikraman cursed. He put

down the unputdownable and opened the door. Gounder.

Vikraman touched Gounder's feet.

Gounder looked pleased. "How are you?"

"Right as a trivet, fit as a fiddle and all that."

"Ah, excellent, excellent," Gounder said and looked around. His eyes fell on the pulp. *The Masked Man and the Volatile Virgin.* "Ah," he groaned.

Vikraman was embarrassed. He stammered: "I… er… thought…" and made an attempt to throw the bed sheet over the paperback.

"Never mind… So, you heard, eh?"

"Yes," Vikraman nodded sympathetically.

Gounder sat down glumly on the bed. "He was like an embroidered bat with red wings. He came out of nowhere. In one bound, he was on top of Manikantan. And in another, he was off him with the necklace."

"It's… it's monstrous! There should be a law against these sorts of things," Vikraman said helpfully.

Gounder fell silent. But his face was expressive. Cogitation ploughed his forehead. "It was as though he knew every move of Manikantan," he said after a space and looked up. "Of course, you wouldn't know anything about it, would you?"

"Who… me? Oh, no. I must have been on the bus by then!"

"Ah, yes… the bus."

"Yes."

"Which one did you take, by the way?"

"What?"

"The bus! Which one did you take?"

"Oh, the bus!"

"Yes, the bus."

"Er… well, the one home."

"The one home! Yes, of course. How silly of me!"

"Not at all. I guess the answer you were looking for was 'great bullfighters can judge a bull by its horns'."

"Ah, that should explain it."

"You know," Gounder began after another space of silence, "there are two kinds of people in this world. The first kind don't give a damn about money. To them, it's all about honour, nobility, and all that. Far as they are concerned, honour once lost is honour lost forever. It cannot be retrieved."

"The second kind don't place so much importance on honour as on money. For them, money once lost is money lost forever. Honour can be retrieved in some form or the other. People have short memories. But money! The one that you recover is never the same as the one that you have lost. You may make more. But it's never the same."

"I belong to the latter. It's not so much the honour as money that troubles me. People are so caught up in their lives that events are forgotten till convenience reminds them."

Vikraman said nothing. He nodded understandingly.

"All this is just by the way," Gounder said with a hollow smile and got up. "Anyway, you rest. We need that leg of yours to be in ship shape for the next tournament," he added.

Vikraman smiled.

"That's another thing," Gounder frowned, regarding Vikraman"'s legs thoughtfully, "it was most curious. But the man… he too had a limp. At first, I thought, that was his style, being Spanish and all. But now that I think about it, he was limping."

"Oh?"

"Of course, you wouldn't know anything about it, would you?"

"Er… bullfighters?" Vikraman shrugged enlighteningly.

"Ah, that should explain it," Gounder said and fixed another thoughtful gaze on Vikraman's leg. "Hmmmm…"

"Very well, toodle-oo," Gounder said.

"Pip pip."

Gounder opened the door.

"Erm…" Vikraman called from behind, rather hesitantly.

"Yes?" Gounder turned around.

"I have a confession to make."

"Confession! What confession?"

"I have wronged you."

"Wronged me! How?"

Vikraman sighed. He dug his hand into his pocket and fished out the emerald necklace.

Gounder looked at it in mock surprise, nodded with satisfaction and looked at Vikraman endearingly.

He sighed in relief and wiped off the few drops of tears that threatened to overflow. "I knew it all along."

"You knew?"

Gounder nodded. He lifted up his shirt and pulled out a tattered, yellowed, dog-eared book from his waist. "*Spanish in Three Months*. Town library. Issued to Vikraman. Returned before due date."

Vikraman hung his head in shame.

"Now now. Let it go. The capers of the youth!"

"You know, there are two kinds of people in this world."

"And you belong to the former."

"Yes, former. Money is ephemeral. But honour, it's eternal."

"To each his own. At least my heirloom is safe. Honour shall be restored next year, eh?"

"Yes," Vikraman said handing over the heirloom.

"Well, all is well that ends well."

Vikraman nodded. "Yes, much ado about nothing."

"Good night."

"Night!"

Gounder opened the door and walked out into the night.

Vikraman closed the door with a sigh and sat down on the bed with a light heart. Gounder has got his money and he his honour. *Excellante*! He smiled and reached under the bed to pull out the cloth mask when he remembered the ravishing ravine that Sheela's malfunctioned sari had revealed like mist off a valley. He whistled a bar of *España Cañí* and reached for the book when he fancied he heard voices outside.

"*¡Caramba*! Gounder hasn't left?" he wondered and peeped through the slit between the curtains.

Gounder hadn't and he wasn't alone. He was with Silamparasan.

"The rascal confessed," he said holding up the necklace. "Not a bad egg after all."

"So?"

"Let it be… No harm done."

"All right," Silamparasan nodded his head in assent and whistled softly into the dark.

Vikraman pressed his head against the windowpane and craned his neck. From the flanks of his house, men emerged and joined the duo before leaving with them. Behind their backs they carried stick swords and brass knuckles.

AN UNBIDDEN GHOST

Someone had to see it. Someone turned out to be Thresyamma. She immediately ran a temperature.

The centenarian's sunken eyes were popping out of their sockets as she narrated it.

"I saw it…! I saw it…!"

"Saw what?"

"Paulie's ghost!"

"What! Where?"

"I was coming back from the fields. It wasn't quite light, but there was a bit of foreglow. I hadn't reached the climb near Varu's house when all of a sudden … along the wall … oh!" Thresyamma pulled the blanket over her and shuddered. "Just the way he was lowered, the shroud and all," she whispered fearfully.

"He stretched his hands towards me and said: 'Thresyammachi… I'm thirsty…!' Oh!" Thresyamma cringed. Her eyes quivered. Then stilled. And she went straight to kingdom come.

Thresyamma was buried the next day at the town cemetery.

"The fossil must have imagined it," someone remarked as the crowd turned away.

"Must have been a cloth in the wind."

"I reckon it was the Lord's way of getting his own back on her for overstaying her welcome."

Chuckle.

"Tut-tut, don't speak ill of the dead."

"These are epiphanies. Paulie was Thresyamma's cousin twice removed."

"It's the widow that I feel sorry for. Paulie hasn't been gone six months and she has to go through this. Poor thing!"

"And so young!"

The last observation put a sudden halt to the conversation, for though the sentiment was in the right spirit, the tone was in the wrong flesh. Everyone looked at the speaker disapprovingly.

"Well, I was just saying," the speaker, name of Thoma, tried to explain innocently.

Others grunted and slowly dispersed.

But in all this, the ghost was clean forgotten. Clearly, nobody gave it much thought. As far as they were concerned, the ghost was a figment of Ms T's imagination. That or a length of cloth caught in the wind.

So, someone else had to see it again for the theory to gain currency as at least a postulation. And it was Thoma, that Good Samaritan who had expressed his sadness over the widow's wasted youth that turned out to be that someone.

He was rumoured to have knocked on the widow's bedroom window in the middle of the night when the ghost appeared and cracked him on the head with a stick. He measured his length on the ground without much fuss and passed out.

When he came to, the villagers knocked him senseless for knocking on the widow's window. Thoma was never seen in the village, again.

But again, the ghost's hand in the whole incident was overlooked. The handiwork was attributed to a coconut.

There is always a third one. It is the third one's testimony that often truly establishes the ghost as a force to be reckoned with.

And it was Vikraman, that dashing young man who had been laughing it all off, that drew the short straw on that one. He had infamously remarked, "Ghosts! What will we hear of next? Aliens? Ha ha ha ha."

It was like this:

Vikraman was returning home from the railway station, having gone to see off someone inconsequential to the story, when it happened.

It was about three in the morning and the way back was along the mile-long path that stretched from the town to the village through the paddy fields.

When the taxi turned in to the said path, Vikraman was suddenly struck by the singular beauty of the night. What with the path lit up by the crescent above and the stars around, the grains swaying in the cool breeze and the gurgle of water rushing through the canal that snaked across the fields, Vikraman was overpowered. 'Nature is best viewed at night,' he concluded, 'unless it's a sunrise, which must be viewed in the morning.' He asked the cabbie to pull over.

The cabbie pulled over and raised a questioning eyebrow.

"It would be a crime not to dive into a night like this," Vikraman elucidated.

"An excellent decision, sir," the cabbie was more then happy to concur. It meant a mile less for him. And he had already been paid. He wished Vikraman the top of the night and drove off.

Vikraman fanned the smoke that eddied from the departing cab away from his face, took a deep whiff of the night air and dove. As he plunged, he wondered: "Does three AM make it night air or morning air?" He weighed the pros and cons and struck out towards home.

It was when he reached the climb at the end of the path - around the same place where the ghost first put in an appearance - that Vikraman noticed a movement.

At first glance, it appeared to be a length of white cloth, caught in a branch, blowing about. At second glance, it became apparent that there was a figure attached to it. At third glance, Vikraman gave a start and stopped dead.

"The… the… ghost!" he stammered weakly. Just as Thresyamma had described it, the shroud and all!

It stretched its hands out towards Vikraman

and echoed in a hollow voice: "Vikraman… I'm thirsty…!"

"Help!" Vikraman screamed and scrammed. He fell down, picked himself up and scrambled up the climb. Once he reached the top, he looked over his shoulder to see if the ghost had taken to chasing him.

But the stretch was empty! There was not a soul in sight, let alone the soulless one. Just a cool breeze blew about.

Vikraman went home straight, complained of a headache and soon ran a temperature. By noon he was shivering and by evening, delirious. The rants were just a matter of time. And the whole affair that he had hoped to keep under wraps came out in fits and starts: "Ghost! Ghost! Water! Mamma! Help!"

The doctor was sent for. The doctor arrived and immediately proceeded to feel the pulse but drew his hand back with an 'ouch!'. Vikraman was red hot. The doctor next went for the thermometer. Mercury shot up cracking the thermometer.

By then, the medicine man was perspiring. He dabbed the beads that formed around his forehead with a handkerchief and got up, scribbled something on the prescription pad and left in a hurry.

The near and dear looked at the slip of paper. Just one word was scrawled across it: 'Kooman'.

Kooman, the local sorcerer!

The sorcerer was sent for. The sorcerer arrived.

The sorcerer placed his palm on Vikraman's forehead and quipped: "Anybody cares for an omelet?" and chuckled at his own joke. The near and dear smiled indulgently. Once he was done with chuckling, the sorcerer called for a glass of fresh milk, unpasteurized.

The glass of fresh milk appeared, unpasteurized. He placed it on Vikraman's forehead and brought it to a boil, reached into his pouch of tricks and took a pinch of grey powder before adding it to the simmering lact. It bubbled over with a hiss. He removed the glass from Vikraman's forehead and let it cool. Then poured the preparation down Vikraman's throat.

Vikraman sputtered and choked and was revived momentarily. He looked around bleary-eyed, saw the sorcerer and said, "what's up, sorc?" faintly before passing out again.

The near and dear let out sighs of relief and

sent up a few prayers.

The sorcerer cocked his mouth satisfactorily and pulled out an amulet. "Charged with a thousand chants," he remarked for everyone's benefit and tied it around Vikraman's right arm.

"Poor sod had a bit of a fright! He'll be all right," the sorcerer explained casually and got up. He collected his *dakshina*[16], lit a beedi and left.

By the next day, fever had come down, although it maintained a steady 104 degrees.

Meanwhile, the village was in a furore over the atrocities of the ghost. Calls for something to be done about it rose. If that was the fate of dashing young men, what would be that of the undashing? If only they had paid heed to Thresyamma! Not that it would have helped. But still... What must they do now? they pondered.

Someone suggested Kooman, the local sorcerer. After all, he was the one who saved the young man from a certain death. The doctor had pronounced him beyond the scope of modern medicine.

---

[16] just like a fee, but non-reimbursable

But since the deceased was a Christian, Father Kurishampalli staked a claim to all matters concerning the ghost. He summoned the good Christians of the parish to the church for a meeting and a prayer.

Since there weren't many Christians in the village and heathens seldom attended church functions as a rule - unless it was a wedding with pineapple slices served at the end of the feast - only a handful turned up.

So, Father Kurishampalli addressed the handful: "Paulie's untimely death was one of the darkest chapters of our serialised lives. A boat that bore twenty little lambs across the serene waters of Thekkady … shepherding them, well, like a shepherd, our Paulie … A sudden engine explosion! It ripped the boat apart. The children were miraculously saved. Praise the Lord!"

"Praise the Lord," the congregation murmured.

"But Paulie who was near the engine with the boatman -," Fr. Kurishampalli paused, "departed for the house of our father in heaven."

The congregation shook its collective head

sympathetically.

"Or so we thought," Fr. Kurishampalli continued. "But Paulie didn't leave us. His spirit still roams the village."

"What happened to that young man is quite unfortunate," he went on. "I hear he was quite dashing. But does that make Paulie's spirit an evil one?"

"No!" Father Kurishampalli answered for everyone, "the church doesn't think so. All he did was ask for a glass of water! Maybe the poor soul thought he could put out the fire that consumed him with a glass of water. It's not his fault that people misconstrue his posthumous intentions and take fright and flight."

"His widow Mary and her little lambs are here. The church has spoken to the ever-grieving widow and has procured her consent to reinter the body with a double dose of mass, our father in heaven and whatnot."

Oh!s and murmurs.

No sooner had he heard the proclamation than Sabu got up, crossed himself and excused himself. He leapt on his bike and was gone like the wind.

He blew over only once he reached the village.

There he went from heathen to heathen asking if they had heard. Naturally they hadn't, since Sabu was the first to have come out of the church. So, he let it be heard.

The news caught on like wildfire and consumed the village in an hour or so. People responded with "what?"'s and "what else?"'s and certain exchanges became quite inevitable.

"Have you heard?"

"I was the first to hear."

"How's that possible? Sabu told me first."

"What do you know? I heard it at the church!"

When Vikraman heard the news, he is said to have taken a deep breath and held it.

The following Sunday was chosen for the groundbreaking event and the churchyard witnessed the biggest congregation in its hallowed history as heathens joined Christians - pineapple slices or not - on compound walls, terraces of nearby shops, belfry and even on the tombs.

Father Kurishampalli arrived looking all important, smiling at the regulars and taunting the irregulars.

"Ah, is that you, Varkey? Been some time, eh? Come to check on the corpse, have you?"

Varkey made some shuffling movements.

Father Kurishampalli passed on and reached the spot. He motioned the gravediggers to begin.

The gravediggers undertook their job as the congregation held its collective breath and looked on. After an hour or so, the earth was removed, and the coffin hauled up. Father Kurishampalli stepped forward and asked the lid to be opened.

The congregation craned its neck and looked.

The lid was raised.

The congregation let out a gasp.

The coffin was empty!

The congregation looked at Father K.

Father K stared back and gulped.

The moment he saw it, Sabu jostled out, leapt on his bike and was gone like the wind. Once he reached the village, he realised that everyone was at the cemetery.

Inspector Uruttu Mathan, who was on hand, slammed his right fist into his left palm and roared: "Those interns from the medical college! Always disrespecting the dead. Bodysnatchers! They'll know that I have something to say about it and they'll hear about it." He leapt into his jeep and tore off.

Nobody paid him any attention.

The sexton suddenly remembered something and piped up. "Now that the cat's out of the can, I recall strange goings-on in the cemetery a few weeks after Paulie's burial."

"What strange goings on?" Fr. Kurishampalli frowned.

"Sounds!"

"What sounds?"

"The sort that the undead crawling out of its hole makes."

"Corroborate."

So, the Sexton mimicked some sounds. Whoosh … Creak … Gaaaw … Gulp! "The last one was mine."

"And you are telling me all this now?" Fr. Kurishampalli scowled.

"I'm an old man. I was scared. I thought it was a ghost."

"You thought it was a ghost! What do you

think now?"

"Now I know it was *the* ghost."

And with that, the ghost became a registered voter entitled to a monthly ration of five kilos of rice and two litres of kerosene.

When Vikraman heard the news, he is said to have let out a sigh!

Soon stories of ghost-spotting began to gain currency in the village, every new story driving a new nail into Vikraman's coffin that his wounded pride was. For the narrators seldom skipped a beat, let alone run a temperature upon sighting the ghost. One even went so far as to narrate an instance where the ghost asked: "Got a light, Ramu?"

Post recovery, Vikraman sat for very many portraits of '*A Young Man Cutting a Sorry Figure*'. The whole thing had left him rather under the weather. A pall of gloom seemed to have fallen over him. Listlessness became his general aspect. He grew a beard and was hardly seen during the day.

Someone saw him at night. "Is that you, Vikraman? I say, don't be out by yourself at night. Didn't you take fright once?"

It was all Vikraman could do from breaking down. He went home straight and shut himself up for good, which didn't help matters since there now lurked the danger of being branded as a perennial rat. And even if he did drum up enough courage to brave the outside world, repressed sniggers threatened to make him a butt.

The ghost became an obsession for Vikraman. Day and night, he thought about it. If only he hadn't gone to see off his friend. If only he hadn't dived into the night. If only more villagers got spooked. If only …"

Sleep became the first casualty. Even if he did catch a wink from sheer somnia, the ghost instantly appeared in his dream and jolted him.

By the time the moon crescented out on the fortnight, Vikraman had decided to banish himself from the village. 'Somewhere far away, where I can re-chronicle my life,' he thought, stroking his beard listlessly.

That night, while his side of the world lost itself in that brilliant phenomenon called rapid eye movement, Vikraman sat up in his bed. He thrust some money into his pocket and stole out of his house.

Outside, the night was as dark as ever. He thanked his lucky stars for the moonless night and walked out into the night like a ghost himself, shadowless.

Grains of soil crunched under his heels softly. A breeze played on his hair and flitted away. Vikraman took it as the last goodbye.

He had to take the lane that had thrown up the ghost to reach the town and when he reached the slope, he stopped and peered, but strangely, not out of fear. If anything, he appeared a tad disappointed. It was as though he had half-expected to see the ghost. He looked around. Nothing.

He walked down the slope. On either side, the paddy fields stretched endlessly till the horizon like black work. He thought about the rains when the fields overflowed spawning countless plantain rafts. That was his fondest memory.

He crossed the canal. That was his land. That was his territory. Suddenly he was overcome with a sort of canine atavism. He wanted to mark it out like a dog by making water.

He slipped under the shadow of a coconut palm and piddled, tracing a semi-circle in the air. He felt relieved. He shook out the last drop and stepped back when he thought he heard a sound coming from far. He glanced towards the village. Something was making its way down along the edge of the path; something bent double, something looking hither and thither, something sticking to the shadows.

Vikraman slipped behind the palm and peered.

The something crept along on all fours, pausing at intervals and glancing over its shoulder. Whatever it was, it was not aware of Vikraman's presence and was headed straight for the palm.

After what seemed like an age, it reached the spot and straightened up slowly, still glancing around and came face to face with Vikraman.

Vikraman gave a start. Paulie's ghost!

The ghost too gave a slight start but recovered in time. It stared at Vikraman for a space. Then it stretched its hands out towards Vikraman and echoed in a hollow voice: "I knew you'd come …!"

But this time Vikraman didn't scream. This time Vikraman didn't scram. This time Vikraman just stared.

Naturally, the ghost wasn't impressed.

"Vikraman," it continued in its hollow voice, "I can't stand it anymore. I'm thirsty…"

Still Vikraman stared.

The ghost next said: "Boo."

"You're not dead!" Vikraman said slowly as though he had trouble coming to terms with the fact.

Paulie smiled. "Why yes! Hallelujah. The Lord be praised."

"And I be damned!" Vikraman gnashed his teeth and collared him.

"Vikraman, please!" Paulie begged.

"Please? Please? Oh, that's rich." Vikraman shook his head. "Because of you, a poor old woman had to cash in her chips –"

"She was long overdue."

"An innocent man had to leave the village –"

"Innocent? He knocked on my bedroom window at night."

"A dashing young man was reduced to a milksop."

"I had no choice…! Besides, you are young.

You'll live it down!"

"Live it down? Live it down? The girls - forget the bloody villagers - but the girls, they never stopped giggling."

"It was a mistake."

"Rectify!"

"How?"

"Fess up!"

"I can't."

"We'll see about that," Vikraman said and pulled Paulie towards the village. "There's nothing like vindication to retrieve lost honour."

"Please! If they come to know, we'll never be able to live in this village. My wife and my children; they will never be spared. The insults! The taunts! And the relief fund will have to be –. I could even be arrested for fraud!" Paulie sobbed.

"But you did commit fraud."

"Theoretically, yes."

"Practically too."

"Think about my family! My wife! My children!" Paulie pled.

"Think about my family which I'll never have,

courtesy of you. And as for a wife, no girl would ever agree to marry me, let alone have my children."

"You are a young man, you have plenty of time to prove your detractors wrong," Paulie implored.

"I want to prove it tonight!"

"Please, my family…," Paulie begged again.

"How the hell are you alive anyhow?" Vikraman asked suddenly.

"Well…"

"Who the hell took your place in the grave?"

"Well…"

"And what the hell happened to the body?"

"It's a long story."

"Make it short."

"Well, ok. So, it's like this…"

"Cut it."

"What?"

"I said shove it."

"Shoved."

"A story ain't good unless there is an audience."

"Vikraman, please…! When I tell you my story, you'll know that my hand was forced."

Vikraman considered, but still looked vicious. Then he relented and looked less vicious.

"Heaven knows it was all a terrible mix up," Paulie said. "And I was caught right in the middle of it. But I guarantee you, I didn't kill anyone. It was like this –"

"Your story doesn't concern me," Vikraman interjected meditatively and lapsed into narrowing his eyes and pinching his lips all the while effecting '*A Portrait of a Brooding Young Man*'.

"My family –"

"Shhh…!" Vikraman cut him short. "Let me concentrate."

Paulie glanced around and crouched while Vikraman concentrated.

"Give me the shroud," Vikraman said at length.

"The shroud?"

"Your shawl! The shroud in Thresyamma's words."

"Oh, the shawl! Here you go."

"Now show me a clean pair of heels."

"What?"

"I said scram!" Vikraman hissed.

Paulie scrammed, on all fours.

Vikraman was left alone. He took a deep breath and looked up at the stars. He was sure a few of them were his lucky ones.

He thanked them and sat under the coconut palm. An hour or three must have passed. The stars were beginning to blink and disappear. The sky was slowly turning grey and the bell of the newspaper man's cycle finally rang in the morning.

Vikraman closed his eyes, rolled over and lay like a man who had passed out.

Minutes later he heard a cry of alarm. The newspaper man was shaking him. "Vikraman … Vikraman!"

But Vikraman didn't respond. He continued to be passed out. The shakings stopped. "Somebody, help!" the newspaper man shouted.

The response was rather quick and presently Vikraman was being shaken by more hands. Somebody sprinkled water on his face.

Vikraman slowly opened his eyes and looked around bleary-eyed. Tens surrounded him.

"What happened?" they asked.

"The ghost…," Vikraman whispered drowsily.

"Went out at night again, did you?" they asked in a tone of admonishment.

"Escaped…" Vikraman continued as if still in a daze and sat up slowly.

"What do you mean, escaped?" they frowned.

"But I managed to snatch the shroud," Vikraman went on, ignoring the question and held up the shawl.

Tens looked at the cloth and shrank back. Gasp!

"Without the shroud, it's invisible. It can't trouble us anymore," Vikraman added with a slow triumphant smile.

There was a collective murmur.

The next instant, the newspaper man snatched the shroud, leapt on his bicycle and pedalled away, waving the shroud above his head and screaming: "Hot news! Hot news!"

Minutes later the whole village was resounding with the thumping exploit of that dashing young man, Vikraman. And more minutes later, they crowded around the ghostbuster and entreated: "Tell us all about it!"

So Vikraman told them all about it: "It was a dark and stormy night…!"

Of course, the entire incident was kept from Paulie's widow.

COUP D'ETAT

The French call it, *coup de foudre* or a stroke of lightning. Effectively love at first sight. And it was so with Vikraman as he set his eyes on Urvashi, the quintessential village belle.

By the time he finished sitting for *The Portrait of a Young Man in Love*, Vikraman concluded, "I must claim her for myself!"

But it wasn't all that simple. She was virgin territory ruled over by a malevolent dictator whose watchful eyes flew sorties dawn and dusk. A dogfight was hardly advisable.

Vikraman mulled over the course of action to be taken.

Finally, after much mulling, he decided. *Coup d'etat!*

Only a *coup d'etat* would do!

Therefore, at the crack of dawn, he marched into enemy territory and called out the despot.

The despot appeared and stood still for his sketch - two bloodshot eyes, an enormous handlebar moustache and a belly that could finish off three

Vikramans in one go and not even belch. He filled the door frame, twirled the ends of his moustache and shot Vikraman an enquiring look.

Vikraman gulped. Suddenly, he felt like a general who had marched in with his troops only to find that they had AWOLed at the last minute.

"Mmm…?" The look turned into sound. Guttural.

Vikraman first threatened his troops with court-martial, then cajoled them with promises of extra rations and iterated the maxim: "To the victor, the spoils". The troops rallied round just in time and Vikraman answered: "*Vikramorvashiyam!*"[17]

"Hmmm," the autocrat nodded thoughtfully, "I get the drift." Then after a contemplative pause: "Being?"

"Vikramadityan II."

"Age?"

"Nubile."

"Qualification?"

"Undying love!"

---

[17] Just like *Romeo & Juliet.* But not so tragic!

"Ready to die?"

"No but may write poetry!"

"Ah, the garden-variety!" the anti-democrat said dismissively. "Plenty out there that profess that sort of love. Can't marry her off to all of them, now can I?"

"No."

"Well?"

"Well…"

"Well?"

"Paddy fields! that yield grains of hue that put gold to shame."

"Rolled or real?"

"Real."

"How many stretches?"

"Like a rubber band, stretch it all you like!"

"Watering?"

"South-west and North-east."

"If one gets delayed?"

"Er…"

"And the other overstays its welcome?"

"Well…"

"Well?"

"Coconut palms! They scrape the skies when the wind blows."

"How many heads?"

"The men are still counting. It may take another month."

"Plucking and de-husking?"

"A strong workforce."

"Vassals or communists?"

"Er… latter."

"Year-on-year increments and bonuses and whatnot?"

"*Noblesse oblige*!"

"Year on year increase of coconut prices?"

"Well…"

"Well?"

"Theatres."

"What, talkies?"

"Yes, cinema halls. Two of them."

"Shows?"

"Morning, noon and night. Throw in a matinee and a dash of blue for the second and you get the picture."

"Indian or Italian?"

"*A la mode.*"

"Ever heard of multiplexes?"

"One-stop show!"

"I hear they are planning one in town. Three screens in one building. *A la carte.*"

"Well, someone must champion tradition."

"Even at the risk of being put out of business?"

"Well…"

"Well?"

"A Tusker!"

"No kidding, really?"

"Really."

"He skids logs?"

"No, he carries the deity during festivals."

"Festivals? Oh, that's a shame!"

"Shame! Why?"

"Isn't that the time they go rogue and trample the mahout?"

"Well, Trivikraman hasn't ever."

"Hasn't ever isn't quite the same as won't ever, is it?"

"Well…"

"In the event, won't the Collector step in, order

the beast to be put down and slap a fine on you for good measure?”

“Well…”

“Well?”

“A secret underground cellar!”

“You don’t say!”

“I do. Strewn with all things encrusted. Like Aladdin’s cave. Built around the time of Tutankhamun the Last. Houses the dark deity with her bejewelled nipples, crystal skulls and sapphire body.”

“You don’t mean the one with a temper?”

“Yes, Kali.”

“Isn’t that a problem?”

“Why?”

“Won’t her temper flare if you so much as lay your little finger on even a tiny stone?”

“Well…”

“Won’t she curse you and your family for seven generations inspiring novels and such? *The curse of the dark deity! The wrath of the bejeweled nipples!*”

“Well…”

“Won’t your children die aborning?”

“Yes… er… possibly…”

"Well?"

"Well…"

"Well?"

"Well…"

Vikraman was beat. The *coup* wasn't going on at all as planned. Worse still, he was running out of powder.

But the malevolent dictator was enjoying himself thoroughly. While he had been aware of the political unrest among the youth over the territory and had kept an eye out for infiltrators, he had hardly expected a *coup*. But the putting down of it seemed easier done than said. In the end, it was all turning out to be nothing more than national day fireworks. He smirked at the callow *generalito* and asked again: "Well?'

"Well…" Vikraman was still thinking.

"Well?"

"Well, a grandchild in ten months," Vikraman proclaimed, struck by a sudden inspiration, a *coup de main*! "One with tiny toes and fingers," he added.

The tyrant was now no longer smiling. His bloodshot eyes flared. His moustache bristled. His muscles twitched. His whole body shook. Then it passed and he suddenly looked old. When he spoke, he spoke in a quivering voice: "Don't trifle with an old man's emotions."

"I'm not!" Vikraman swore.

"All right then," he sighed. "Meet me at the temple tomorrow at six. I'll give her away to you."

Vikraman let out a sigh of relief.

The *coup* was over. The dictatorship was overthrown. Nevertheless, the *coup de grace* was delivered by the old dictator - to himself. As Vikraman vaulted over the gate and put a spring in his step, the old guard asked in an unsteady voice: "You won't cheat, will you?"

THE TRANSMUTATION

As Vikraman stirred in his sleep one unfine morning, he found that he had transmuted into a log. His body; that smooth, brown, toned masterpiece that used to set the hearts of village belles aflutter - as he was wont to think - was now a shapeless trunk. Where his hands used to be, there protruded two frail dried branches, while his legs were a tangle of roots, shrivelled and unmovable.

Vikraman gave a start. Figuratively. For being a log, it was impossible to do so literally.

'What happened to me?' he wondered. He could make neither branches nor roots of it.

He looked around. He was lying on his bed in his room. It was not a large room, but capacious enough to accommodate a bed, a study table, a deckchair that he had set right under the window and a bookshelf that flanked the wall to his right. Above the bookshelf was a centrefold that he had taken from a magazine and stuck on the wall. It showed a woman in her birthday suit standing with her back against a wall and smiling mischievously at the spectator.

Everything was as it had been except for him who was not as he had been.

'It must be a dream,' he thought. 'What else could explain it? Whoever heard of transmuting into a log! How about sleeping a little longer and forgetting all this nonsense?' he thought and closed his eyes.

But this seemed easier thought of than done. Not so much on account of his new state as on account of the din from the kitchen.

His room was right next to the kitchen and the noise from the kitchen was only getting louder. There was the sound of chillies and mustard sputtering in the oil, the sound of coconut being grated, the tapping of the spatula on the pan as well as other sundry culinary sounds. Then there was the tantalizing smell of Masala Dosa wafting through the gap in the wooden shelf that was built into the wall between his room and the kitchen. And the shelf was right behind the headboard of his bed.

'It's impossible to sleep with this din in the background!' Vikraman exclaimed. 'Anyone might think there is a battle raging behind these walls.'

'Maybe if I bury my head under the pillow, I

will be able to drown out the sound,' he thought. But no sooner had he thought so than Vikraman felt a wave of shock course through him. 'I have two dried branches for hands. I cannot even move them, let alone pick up the pillow!' he despaired.

'But I must go back to sleep somehow,' he decided at length. 'That's my only hope. With some luck I might wake up as a human being.'

'If I change my position and try to sleep on my left side, I might just go off to sleep,' he thought. It has often worked on those sleepless nights. 'But - how am I to do that? I cannot use my hands. And I don't even want to try using my legs.'

He took a tentative peek at his legs. The dead tangle of roots reminded him of those macabre illustrations of trees one found in gothic fiction. He shrank back in horror. For all intents and purposes, he was just a log of wood. And that was all there was to be said about it.

'What if I rock my body sideways? Why, that might just do the trick! I don't require my hands or legs for that. I just have to rock my body a bit. Just a fraction of a movement and I can build on it thanks to my cylindrical proportion. At any rate, it's worth a shot!' he thought and tried to rock his body sideways.

Surprisingly this worked. Only too well.

'Goodness! I am rolling off the bed!'

Luckily Vikraman's roots hooked around the bars of the bed frame and stopped his sideward spiral.

By then Vikraman was fully awake. There was no going back to sleep now.

'Maybe I should get up and ascertain the situation,' he thought. 'If I can roll off the bed, then who is to say that I can't get up? All it requires is some will power. One must treat it like one of those dreams where one feels pinned down to the bed. One tries to open one's eyes. One can't. One tries to call out for help. One can't. Then one finally wills one's eyes open and gets up.'

Vikraman tried to will himself up, although to all appearances he was just lying on the bed immobile.

'My god! I truly am a log. And as a log I have no mobility except rolling sideways. Couldn't I have transmuted into, say, an insect?'

At that moment, as though adding an exclamation point, he heard his mother call him from the kitchen.

"Ramy, it's almost eight. Get up, now. The tea's getting cold."

'Mother!' In his consternation, he had forgotten that there were other people in the house.

'Yes mother. In a moment, mother. I'm just getting up, mother,' Vikraman replied or rather meant to. But his voice seemed to have developed a woodenness that weighed his words down and sent them crashing to the floor. What came out was: 'Ngummmmmmmn.'

'Ngummmmmmmn?' Is that all he was capable of saying? Vikraman felt another wave of shock course through him. What other horrors awaited him?

But after the initial alarm, he thought about it calmly. 'Maybe if I speak slowly, pronouncing each letter, I might be able to avoid the effect.'

'Let me try again. A syllable at a time. Yes - ma - dur. Just three syllables.'

Vikraman tried saying 'yes'. But what came out was another inarticulate sound. He tried saying 'ma'. This seemed to come out right. Now for 'dur'. This one fell with a dull thud on the floor. Vikraman decided not to say anything anymore. 'It's better if I don't answer. At worst, they would think I'm still asleep, that's all.'

He thought about the time when his mother used to come to wake him up. He would lift his fingers up indicating 'five more minutes'. She would smile, smoothen out his hair, pat his cheeks and leave.

'My god, what if she walks in now? The poor woman would faint … or not. She'd probably think that I've played a prank on her. Or would she think that the joke's gone too far?'

'Probably she'd get angry and put the log in the oven without realizing that it's her own son. She still uses the old oven and firewood at times.'

'No, mother wouldn't do that. She'd probably place it on a chair next to the dining table and carry on, expecting me to come back when I'm hungry to say things like "but, who are you? My son? It can't be. He's already here. See, that's him at the table having his breakfast. Oh, don't mind him, he's a bit of a blockhead" and try to stretch the game a little.'

Vikraman smiled at this.

"When is this boy going to get up?" He heard his mother speak again. She was talking to his sister.

"He was supposed to go out to buy milk. Finally, your father went. His face was swollen as though it were stung by a bee."

'Father!' Vikraman thought with a shudder. He had promised his father that he would go to the cooperative in the morning to buy milk. His uncle and aunt had called to say that they would be dropping in. And his mother had decided to make rice pudding. 'Oh, what would happen when father returns and finds out that I am not up yet?'

His father was the kind that had no patience for human frailties. He expected everyone to be his own man, even little children. Now, he would be back and won't even utter a word, casting a cloud over the entire household.

He often had dreams about his father. They were always the same dream. He saw him lying flat across a map of the world. Sometimes, he had a toothbrush moustache and looked a lot like Hitler and sometimes a heavy one like that of Stalin and at times he appeared in a bicorn[18].

---

[18] Napoleon, in case you are wondering. Napoleon still even if you aren't.

'*He* wouldn't think twice before putting me in the oven,' Vikraman thought. 'He would say that the nonsense - not joke - has gone too far and might even chop me to pieces for good measure before putting me in the oven.'

'Me in the oven!' Vikraman shuddered at the thought. It was tough shuddering being what he was. But he did his best. 'When they miss me, they would search for me. But I would be ashes by then. Ashes to ashes, as they say.'

'And when the fire has died, Chimban would trot in and lie in the ashes. Maybe he would realize that the ashes were me. They say cats are clairvoyant. He might probably cry, and sister would think that it's sighing for milk and pour some in a saucer before brushing the ash off his back. And that would be the end of me. And no one would ever be any the wiser.'

Vikraman sighed.

'But then, how will they open the door?' he wondered. He had lately developed the habit of bolting the door from inside. 'They will have to break the door down.'

'"He had better wake up by the time I'm back'

was what your father said before he left," his mother was saying. "He'd be back soon. Go wake your brother up. If he sees him at least helping in the kitchen, it would save us all a lot of trouble."

"I'm not going," his sister refused. "He would clip me on the ear for waking him up."

'My poor sister. She's afraid that I would clip her on the ear. She doesn't know that her brother's wooden heart has metastasized and turned his entire body into a block of wood. But now, oh, how she's going to miss his temper!'

'My sweet sister. She can play the veena. The other day there were three guests in the house and she played the veena. How they applauded!'

At that moment he heard a knock on the door. "Ramy, are you going to get up or not?" It was his mother. "Your father would be along any time soon. And the last thing he would want to see is you still in bed."

Vikraman made no answer.

"What's with this boy? I have never known him to sleep this late. I hope he's not ill," he heard his mother mutter as she went back to the kitchen. "Oh, let him wake up when he wants to!"

Vikraman fell to thinking about what must be done about the issue at hand when he heard a rumble. It was faint but unmistakable like the drone of impending doom.

'Father! That's the sound of his scooter. He must be turning into the drive.' Vikraman held his breath. He remembered how as a child, the sound of his scooter used to send shudders down his spine, as though his father were actually riding up and down his spinal cord. Even today, a sort of dread came over him whenever he heard the sound of his scooter.

He heard it approaching followed by the metallic clang of the gears changing down. The motor idled and died. Presently he heard his father's feet on the carpet outside. He had paused outside his door and passed on.

'What is going to happen now?' Vikraman wondered.

"Is he not up yet?" He heard his father ask his mother.

"I'm tired of trying to wake him up. By the way, we needed some carrots. I forgot to tell you."

His father made no answer.

Vikraman pricked his ears up. Pin drop. As expected. A little later he heard his father's feet on the coarse carpet again.

"Ramy…" There was a knock on the door.

Vikraman's mind raced. He thought of saying 'Yes, father, I am getting up, father. I'm sorry I couldn't get up earlier and get milk. I wasn't feeling particularly well. I think I am running a temperature. Could you check, please? Thank you. Oh, and I think you look quite dapper in this blue shirt.'

But before he could muster enough courage to even attempt to say all of that, he heard his father's feet leaving the carpet.

'What will happen now?' Vikraman wondered. 'Maybe -'

There was a sound outside his window. The next instant, it flew open. His father stood there with a bucketful of water in his hands. Without a word, he threw the water inside.

Vikraman leapt up. He could move!

"Stop sleeping like a log and get up, you lazy oaf!" his father thundered.

A NIGHT IN THE HILLS

A night in the hills was not Vikraman's idea. It was Loman's.

The local SI was an old buddy of Vikraman from town who had taken it upon himself to prove the astrologer right - the stargazer had predicted that the snotter-in-knickers would be a robbers' nightmare - and flexed his way into pressed Khakis as a constable before double promoting himself to Sub-inspector.

Call of duty had taken him away from his homeland and now the same call put him back in charge of homeland security. SI Loman, soon to be promoted to Inspector.

With a police jeep, a service revolver and two constables to salute him at every turn, Loman felt quite contented and at peace with the world.

Simply put, he was in the mood for a few beers and some game. And what better place than the hills to do just that?

Therefore, one Saturday afternoon, at around three, Loman tore down the sleepy hollow in his jeep. The groggy hamlet sat up with a start and rubbed its eyes. A police jeep? In the village? There's something rotten here!

It followed the stench and fetched up outside Vikraman's house.

The police jeep was parked outside all right, the cop presumably inside, doubtless slapping a pair of handcuffs on the felon.

"I always knew that boy was up to something. Now I know, it was no good!" somebody remarked.

"But what has he done?" somebody else asked on everybody's behalf.

"Heard he carved him up with a jackknife," somebody else yet answered for everybody's benefit.

"Carved up who?"

"The dead one, of course!"

"Oh!"

Soon the jackknife turned into a pistol, the country-make, the one that fires seven rounds; one more than what the police carry. So, the dead one wasn't carved up after all, rather shot, twice in the chest although it came to light pretty soon that the dead one wasn't quite dead but being attended to in the ICU of the city hospital. And the poor soul was none other than their own Jayaraman. But Jayaraman said that that was most curious considering he was standing right next to them at that very moment. Maybe it was the other Jayaraman, he opined. There was another Jayaraman. But then, that's exactly what the other Jayaraman had said too. It was all very confusing.

So, they hung around the house on tenterhooks.

Suspenseful minutes crawled by.

Finally, the lawman emerged with the outlaw.

"Why is he not in uniform? And where are the handcuffs?"

"A poor attempt at a cover up. Out of deference to the family. He knows the lad. Went to the same school and all."

"Pah! Who are they kidding?"

Vikraman looked at his countrymen remorsefully and got into the jeep. Loman hid a smile under his turned-up moustache and sat behind the wheels before driving away.

By the time the jeep painted a miniature of the village in its rear-view mirror, Vikraman had a stash of brown sugar, had molested a girl and was actually a convict on parole whose who went by the alias Raka.

The jeep left the village behind, left the town behind and hit the road that wound around the hills.

Vikraman sat in the jeep fiddling with the SI's service revolver, occasionally making faces and miming a few imaginary tough guy roles.

"Will you put that away?" Loman asked glancing nervously at Vikraman's itchy fingers.

"Why don't I put you away, punk?" Vikraman asked in a deep, faux-Eastwoodian voice.

Loman rolled his eyes.

Vikraman smiled self-indulgently. "Do you know what my ultimate fantasy was?"

"Mrs. Menon?"

"Wild West! Like the man with no name." Vikraman whistled the Moriccone, trained the gun on Loman and said: "Bang!"

The jeep climbed the hill, wound its way up and pulled up along a ledge.

Vikraman and Loman got out of the jeep and stretched their respective limbs.

"You can see the world from here," Vikraman remarked looking down from the ledge. "As long as you believe the world comprises a little village and a littler town."

"Let's take in the scenic later," Loman replied. "We must begin the hunt while we have sun. I hear the place is swarming with rabbits," he said and took his air gun from the jeep.

One look at the air gun and Vikraman could see rabbits piling up at his feet in no time. He snatched the gun from Loman. "Let me show you a thing or two about rabbit shooting," he said and set off with an "after me". Loman shook his head helplessly and followed his trigger-happy friend.

Vikraman flattened himself on the ground behind a thicket and waited while Loman crouched behind another clump and looked on.

A few minutes later, Vikraman was rewarded with the sight of a big white rabbit nibbling whatever it was nibbling.

"Grass," Vikraman concluded and took aim.

The rabbit looked up.

Vikraman squeezed the trigger.

The rabbit scooted.

"You missed!" Loman threw up his arms.

"It looked at me," Vikraman whispered, looking like a man who had just seen a ghost.

"What?"

"The rabbit, it looked at me," Vikraman rolled over and sat up.

"My foot! Gimme the gun," Loman took the gun back from Vikraman. "And by the way, that's when you shoot it between the eyes, when it looks at you. Now you can retrieve for the rest of the evening."

"His name was Keechu," Vikraman said in a daze.

"Oh, shut up!" Loman pushed Vikraman away and skulked about till he found another spot. Vikraman followed him hesitantly, looking half the man he used to be.

Loman took position while Vikraman watched from behind some bushes.

A movement to the left. Loman's eyes darted while his hands brought the gun up.

Vikraman looked away. Loman shot down the rabbit.

Vikraman looked away. Loman shot down another.

Vikraman looked away. Loman shot down one more.

"Now, that's what I'm talking about," Loman said, pointing at the lot.

When Vikraman looked at the dead rabbits, he was moved to tears. Finally, he took heart from the fact that they died for a cause. He thought about the hissing sound they would make on the spit and licked his lips. Their deaths won't go in vain; he swore!

A quarter of an hour later the fire was crackling and the rabbits were making the hissing sound.

Loman brought the icebox from the back of his jeep. Inside it, bottles of beer waited in a cold sweat. The cop collared two and stood them next to each other before turning one over to Vikraman.

The two friends clinked their bottles and took a gulp. Two gulps. Three gulps. A bottle. Two bottles. Time ceased to exist.

The spent bottles huddled together on one side while fleshless bones collected around them.

The two friends reminisced about their fascinatingly misspent youth, laughed on everything, abused the system and discussed the state of the nation.

In between they bickered. Loman threatened to lock Vikraman up in the town jail. Vikraman said he would hang himself in the cell and effect his dismissal. Finally, Loman decided to let him off the hook - for the time being.

The moon shone down upon the two friends.

Vikraman looked up, studied the 'effect' and observed: "Da sheleshtial flashlight!"

Loman grunted and smiled.

"I'm filled with inshpiration," Vikraman declared. "I want to shing."

"Shing," Loman encouraged.

Vikraman howled at the moon and sang:

"Shining shining shilver moon

How I wonder whatcha doon

Up above da world sho high

Like a platter in da shky!"

Loman frowned. "Ish that how it goesh?" he asked.

"How da hell elsh ish it shupposhed to go?"

"Der's a shtar involved shomewhere."

"Oh, der are all shorts of regional vershions."

"Ish der one about da shun too?"

Vikraman thought for a second. "Yup."

"How doesh it go?"

Vikraman collected his thoughts.

"Blazhing blazhing yellow shun

I hear your kind der is none

Up above da world sho high

Like da yolk of a bullsheye!"

Loman said nothing. He reached for the bottle.

"Do you think I'm shlurring?" Vikraman asked after a space.

"Shay shomething."

"She shells she shells on da she shore."

"Nope."

"I didn't think sho either. You know I can drink anyone under da table," Vikraman boasted. "Once I wash vishiting my uncle. Ex-military. You know da kind. A brewtotaller. Had da habit of downing a peg or two after dinner. One for da bed, he ushed to shay. He ashked me if he should pour me one. I shrugged reluctantly. I wash a bit awkward. Hish being old and all. He took it for fear. 'Don't worry, neph,' he said shtroking hish white whishkers with a condeshcending shmile, 'it'sh Vodka. It'sh never known to have killed anyone except da Russiansh.' He chuckled and poured a shmall. 'It will put hairs on your chest,' he shaid and reached for da diluter. Water. But I put my hand out and shtopped him. He looked up with surprise. I shrugged apologetically, picked up da glash and downed da Russian ash if he were a Mexican, took a piece of lime, crushed it on my tongue and shook my head. I wiped my lipsh and looked up. He wash shtaring at de empty glash in my hand. It stayed on it for a while and den went back to hish. You wouldn't have shushpected it contained vodka even if you had tashted it. It wash all cola and ice. I don't think he finished hish drink.''

Loman guffawed and recalled a similar instance while Vikraman got up and looked for a spot to make more room for the remaining beers.

Loman continued to recount his exploit while Vikraman continued to make room. That's when Vikraman fancied he heard a sound.

He turned around and looked at Loman. It wasn't Loman. Not that Loman wasn't making sounds under the pretext of talking. But that wasn't him.

Since his eyes were half-closed, narrowing

them to concentrate was not a viable option. So Vikraman closed them and pricked his ears up. Sounds, all right! Muffled and from far.

"Hey," Vikraman called out softly to Loman. "Whashat shound?"

"That'sh you making water."

"Not dat."

"Oh, that'sh me talking."

"Not you."

"Now it'sh you. Now it'sh me."

"Not ush!"

"Den?"

"Jusht come here, will you?"

"Gimme a moment," Loman said making a grunting effort to get up. "What shound?" he lurched over and ashked.

"Hear dat?"

"Who da…!"

"Shhh…"

"Wha?"

"Shoftly!"

Loman covered his mouth and said: "Musht be catsh on heat."

Vikraman considered for a moment. "No. I shay, lesh inveshtigate".

"Hold on. Lemme gedda gun. If it'sh a boar, we cud zhap him," Loman said and went to get his gun but returned with a flashlight.

"Ok, now shhh…," Vikraman cautioned his friend and tiptoed forward.

"Shhh…" Loman agreed and tiptoed after Vikraman.

"Keep to da hard shoil," Vikraman instructed.

Loman kept to the hard soil.

"Ash sure-footed ash a mountain goat."

"Maybe it'sh a mountain goat!" Loman brightened up.

"Shhh…" Vikraman shushed Loman and traced the sound. It seemed to come from behind a clump of bushes, a bit far off and down a slope.

It was a tricky descent. But they made it as safely and quietly as they could. Once they were near the bushes, Vikraman paused and listened.

"Are you thinking whad I'm thinking?" he asked Loman in a whisper.

"Whad are you thinking?" Loman whispered

back.

"You know…"

"No."

"Bushwhackers."

"What's that?"

"Bang bang!"

"Bang bang? You mean it'sh really a boar?"

"No!"

"Den?"

"Bang, bang! Boy-on-girl action! Shavvy?"

Boy - girl - action. Words circled round Loman's head like homing pigeons and finally struck home. He wash shavvy indeed! Only too well.

His eyes flared. The gallons vapourised. The good cop took leave off him and in came the bad cop - Local SI, Loman, soon to be promoted to Inspector. He parted the bushes and roared: "Who da hell ish making out in da bushesh of my preshinct?" and pulled the trigger. The beam shot out of the flashlight and fell on four bulbous, terrified eyes; an unclad woman and a semi-clad youth.

"Coitush interruptsh," Vikraman soliloquised.

The next instant, the boy clutched his clothes

and vanished in a trail of his fluttering mundu[19].

Vikraman and Loman returned their male gazes to the reclining nude.

"That'sh one hell of a birthday shuit," Vikraman remarked.

"Haute couture!" Loman couldn't agree more.

The birthday girl rose slowly and stood bathed in the flashlight. She regarded Vikraman and Loman from under her lashes. Then tossed her hair lightly and said nonchalantly: "Five hundred per head.

---

[19] Just like a lungi but spelt differently.

Also by this Author

THE TIGER HUNT

WHEN A VILLAGE IS HELD TO RANSOM BY A TIGER, THE VILLAGERS BRING IN A HUNTER TO SNARE THE CAT. BUT AS THE CAT AND MOUSE GAME STARTS, IT BECOMES QUITE UNCLEAR AS TO WHO THE FIGURATIVE CAT IS. LACED WITH HIS USUAL WIT AND WORDPLAY, THE TIGER HUNT IS ARGUABLY GIRI KURICHIYATH'S FINEST WORK SO FAR AND A PERFECT COMPANION TO WICKERMAN CAPERS.